MW01274281

Taiwan Tales

One Country, Eight Stories: A Multicultural Perspective

Katrina A. Brown
J.J. Green
Amanda Miao
L.L. Phelps
CK Hugo Chung
Tony Messina
Edward Y. Cheung
Patrick Wayland

Lone Wolf Press
Cover Photo by Craig Ferguson
craigfergusonimages.com

Contents

When a burned-out American baseball player is offered a chance to play for a team in Taiwan, he gets one last chance to redeem himself on the field and learn why his life has gone so wrong.

Can one expat eat his way out of a nervous breakdown?

Jia-ying decides to break a few 'nonsensical' traditions of Ghost Month. But some ghosts don't care if they're believed in as long as they get their revenge.

In a damaged future where people trade in forgotten technology, one man collects something much more valuable.

He knows pursuing a romance during his compulsory military service is risky. But there is no turning away from what the heart desires.

Lara, a seer for magical creatures, has escaped to the other side of the world. Yet no matter how far she runs, she can't escape her destiny.

Overpopulation has become unmanageable in the port city of Keelung. Don't worry. The government has a solution.

A young American's flirtatious fling with the city of Taipei.

Roger Jergenson's Flyout

by
Patrick Wayland

I'll let you in on a little secret: incandescent is dead. Doesn't matter the reason. Compact fluorescent bulbs are the king. Long live the king. Sam Fillmore, by the way, VP of light bulb sales, very nice to make your acquaintance. When I saw you sitting over here at the bar, I said to myself, 'Sam, there's a fellow traveler with a couple hours to waste. Why don't you go make yourself comfortable in that seat next to the only person at the bar?' My mother used to say, 'Make friends or make trouble.'

Can I buy you a drink – or another? Visited Taipei before? I'm here every three months to check in at the factory. Have to keep up to date on product. Originally from Boise, Boise, Idaho – haven't been back in two years. I swear these hotel maitre D's know me better than my own mother. 'Your usual T-bone and baked potato, Mr. Fillmore? And your glass of house red with that?' You can probably tell from my figure, I'm a meat and potatoes man.

What's that? Just here to watch the game. Not interested in chatting? That's fine with me. Baseball's my favorite sport; after all, I'm an American too. I gather you already know the Taiwanese are crazy about it. You think *we're* fans? Well, let me show you something. Take a look at this bill here in my wallet. You see that? That's their little league baseball champions. That's how much they love the sport. They put a baseball team on their money. What's that? Never knew that, huh? Well, I'll tell you another story you might not have heard. Ever hear of Roger Jergenson? Oh, well, sure you know him now as the big hitter for Cincinnati – bats about three-ninety, career RBIs over eight hundred, in the All-Stars last year, as I recall. But I'll wager you didn't know who he was five years ago. Well, five years ago I did know him, and I'm in no way bragging when I say this because if you knew him then, you'd say he was a real son-of-a-biscuit – excuse my French. And I'll double-or-nothing my bet that you didn't know it was some little Taiwanese girl who turned him around.

How did I know him? Well, he was playing

for a team right here in Taiwan. Used to drink in this very bar. As you may know he started out playing for Tampa Bay. Was there exactly two years and twelve days before they dropped him mid-season because he couldn't get on base. Every one of his hits was a fly-out, aimed for the fence. Then his agent dropped him. He'd lost his sparkle as we say in the sales business. And he fell into a pool of players waiting to be picked up in the Triple-A league. Four months later, his wife left him – that didn't really hit him hard until later. At the time he didn't believe she was sacrificing enough for his best interests.

Well, a couple weeks later, he got this call from a manager here for one of the national teams. This manager, in his broken English, said they could use a hitter and wanted to give him a chance because of his early record. Jergenson spent one sleepless night thinking it over real hard. He'd never stepped one single foot outside the forty-eight states, didn't much care for foreigners. But he knew he needed to play. That was the only thing that mattered – stepping back out on that field, gripping the pine. He needed to get back into a game. A neglected skill's no different than a neglected factory machine – after a time, they both rust and stop working. You know what it's called when a player drops out of the majors for six months? Retirement. Jergenson didn't even know where Taiwan was, but he signed that contract the next day and faxed it back.

So, there he was, one major league dropout – no pun intended – stepping off the plane onto this Asian island, knowing nothing except that it was his last shot. Well, as you may know, these Taiwanese are all about the appearance of professionalism. They picked him up in a limo, started him out in that four-star hotel across the street before moving him into his luxury apartment, got someone to take him around and show him the sights. The coach for that team was a man named Ken Wu. He was about sixty at the time, but as fit as someone half his age. Still got out there and hit the outfield practice flies. Learned his baseball from the Japanese and followed their training regimens which I can explain in three words: drills, drills and drills. And unlike the young players, he was the only one who knew English well enough to talk much with Jergenson without the translator they hired.

Now, Jergenson appreciated those rote drills. He saw them as a refresher course. To him it felt like baseball boot camp all over again. And when that first game started, he was ready to knock that ball off the island. Well, number two got on first. With one out, Old Wu gave the signal for him to bunt. Bunt??? That's what Jergenson was thinking. Taiwanese baseball parks look a lot smaller than American ones. The stands are smaller, but the field is regulation, the length is no different. The crowd for the opposing team was standing, filling the stadium with cries, whistles and sounds from their noise-makers to disrupt the batter. Jergenson's blood burned hot, he needed to let loose, kill it, send it out of the stadium. So he shook off Mr. Wu's signs. Mr. Wu signaled again, this time more emphatically. Sacrifice bunt! The team needed that runner on second base. But Jergenson didn't lower his bat. He needed to win that game. He needed to show all those people that dropped him that he could do it. He needed to show himself most of all and he didn't believe any of the other players could help accomplish this important goal. The first pitch was thrown, right up the middle and a little low. His sweet spot. He twisted with everything he had. Crack! and that ball—

Look at that! We missed a double play on the TV. And wasn't that your team that made it? What's the score? Top of the seventh. Perhaps I talk too much. My mother used to say, 'Better to put a fork in your mouth than a foot.' You ready for another drink? Certainly, I'll tell you what happened, if you want. Where was I? That's right, the first game. The start of Roger Jergenson's comeback.

But it didn't happen. He sent that ball flying up, up, up. It must have had a record height on it. When it fell, it fell nice and easy – might as well have been on a parachute – it fell straight into the centerfielder's glove. In that one fly-out, Jergenson's belief in his abilities and who he was collapsed like one of those buildings they demolish with explosives. When he returned to the dugout, he broke his bat over the steel railing. Later, after the game, he got into an argument with the coach about the team's need for his hitting. And if you understand this culture, you understand that arguing with a superior at your job is as bad as arguing with your church preacher. It's just not done.

His teammates tried to talk to him, make him feel at home. They invited him out for dinner and drinks, but he never accepted. Jergenson spent his time inside his apartment or at the American bar next door, turning his back on anyone trying to speak to him. During this time he found much to complain about. The jostling crowds, the taxis honking at him, the heat, local dishes having too much soup and too little meat, the mopeds that people drove carelessly down the sidewalks, the mix-ups caused by language barriers. Funny story – he once ordered a hamburger with extra mayo, but got bread without meat. You see the word mayo sounds like the Chinese word for 'without.' Mayo and beef must have been misinterpreted to 'without beef.' It's a funny mistake, but when you're hopeless, those small things add up, can make you go mad.

It was Mr. Wu who came to Jergenson one afternoon, after watching a third disastrous loss, and said they were going out. Wu told Jergenson to leave his wallet behind, he didn't need any money. Now, I think you've at least read about the gentlemen's clubs here. Two beautiful women for every man at the table. Others serving top-shelf cocktails. Jergenson had that in mind as they headed out in Wu's car. Jergenson's thoughts drifted from remembering his bachelor party to images of oriental massages while Wu talked about team spirit and relying on his friends. Jergenson didn't even take note as they left the skyscrapers of the city behind and moved out into the rice paddies. Jergenson figured he was ready for a wild night out with the only person in the country he felt comfortable with. For three hours they drove, passing betel trees, glassy rice fields and red brick houses, discussing the game, sometimes arguing, sometimes agreeing. Finally in some village at the foot of some mountain, Wu stopped the car. Jergenson asked where the nightclub was. Wu replied they weren't there for that. Confused, Jergenson got out of the car and looked around for a baseball field or sports center. He asked, 'Why are we here?' Wu replied: 'I brought you here to learn something.' And then, with the sun just starting to set over the mountain, Wu started to drive away, back up the road they had come from, soon disappearing behind a cluster of banyan trees.

What did Jergenson do? He laughed. He stood there in the middle of the road, which was nothing but packed dirt, and laughed, sure that Mr. Wu would turn around, come back and get him. He waited ten minutes before sitting down. After twenty minutes, the sun had fully set, the clear sky darkened and the summer air cooled slightly. After forty minutes, he finally saw the light and knew Mr. Wu was not coming back, and so he stomped up that road toward a group of low structures.

Oh, the things he imagined doing to that Mr. Wu. He wanted to wring his neck with his own two hands. Who the heck did that Mr. Wu think he was, and what kind of spit-ball trick was he trying to pull? The path turned into a one-lane paved road that rambled through the small village. The stars were out above a few clouds now, and Jergenson worried about the neighborhood as he looked for a taxi. Then he remembered, reaching to touch his back pocket, he didn't have his wallet. In fact, he didn't have a single dollar on him.

What's that? You want to know about the little girl? Well, hold your horses, I'm getting there, I'm getting there.

Where was I – oh yeah – Jergenson started looking around for street signs. With Mr. Wu driving he hadn't seen which direction they had headed much less which streets they'd passed. But of course in the country everything's in Chinese. All those characters made as much sense as chicken scratch to him. He could hear the muffled sounds of people talking, radio music, children laughing behind glowing windows. He could smell and hear foods being fried – the scratch of the spoon against the wok. And this got his stomach grumbling because he'd only eaten a late brunch.

Well, now, I have to admit something. Maybe you figured it out already, but I don't miss many meals, and I've heard that empty stomachs can make people do things they might not do when they feel all filled up and comfortable. Some people say there's a desperation or panic that takes over when one doesn't know where that next meal is coming from. Fortunately, I have never felt that, but that's what Jergenson was feeling as he turned around in a circle, lost, hungry and helpless. For an hour he walked the streets. At one point he came upon some men sitting around a low table, drinking. He quickly turned around and went the other way. He didn't know what they were up to – they might try to kidnap and ransom him. Up another street an old woman pushing a cart stacked with bags started talking to him in her foreign tongue, making no sense, so he jogged away from her. He found a wide avenue and followed it for a while. The houses there were strange to him, the living rooms opened up onto the street like a garage should. He quickly passed these little pockets of life so the families inside wouldn't get suspicious.

After another hour, his stomach was gripped in a knot of pain. He usually ate a good sized dinner, and it was like his body was demanding what it always got. He passed convenience stores, but without a coin what would he buy? Then as the avenue ran along the flat, dark field of a rice paddy, he saw a banana tree with its fruit hanging. It was just inside a low wall and under a street light. The bananas were green, but large, ripe. He walked up the street, looking up at this find like manna from heaven. Without a thought, he jumped the knee-high wall, quickly broke off one of the bananas and in one move stepped back over onto the road. He made himself comfortable on that wall, peeled down the skin, exposing that wonderful, fragrant, delicious fruit and bit off a chunk. Thinking it was the best banana he had ever tasted, he finished it off in seconds. He sat there enjoying that substance hitting his stomach, still holding the green peel in his hand with his eyes half closed when he caught the smell of smoke in the air.

Where did the smoke come from? Oh, the smoke was from a cigarette. He turned and saw that he was being watched, an old man puffing on a cigarette that glowed red in the shadows of the house. Jergenson didn't move, wondering how long the man had been there. Then the old man started talking, quietly at first, stepping out from under the awning. His words were sing-song, but warm. He walked over to the banana tree, continuing this one-way conversation that Jergenson couldn't understand a single word of. Then he reached up and broke off one, two, three, four bananas, the cigarette dangling from his lips. He turned, Jergenson stood, wondering how much trouble he was in, as they faced each other from across the low wall. The old man held out the fruit, nodded and spoke in his tongue, probably not even speaking Chinese, but the local dialect of Taiwanese as they do in the country. Well, as I can tell you, one banana does not a meal make. Jergenson knew he would need more. Feeling embarrassed and ashamed at having stolen from some poor old farmer,

Jergenson, head bent, took the gift, and quietly walked back up the street to the avenue.

He sat at a bus bench and ate his dinner, watching a woman feeding ghost money into a blazing caldron across the street. Above him more clouds raced by. I'm sure you've seen that Taiwan is one of those few places where your umbrella can become your parasol and your parasol can become your umbrella in less than an hour. It is an island after all. Well, in a short time, fat drops began hitting the pavement, and Jergenson, pulling in his feet under the bus stop's cover, mulled over his helpless situation. Even if he did get a taxi, how would he tell the driver where to go? The rain came down hard now, falling like a curtain around his little space. He found the bus schedule and could make out a timeline with regular numbers, and it looked like the last bus had passed almost an hour earlier. Across the street, the woman had finished her praying and was gone. At that hour the streets were mostly empty except for the occasional passing truck. Jergenson rubbed a chill off his arms. The rain was splashing up and hitting him. Then through that curtain of water appeared the woman who had been across the street. She was holding two umbrellas. One she used, the other was closed. She started talking to him. Again he couldn't make out heads from tails about what she was saying, but it was clear she was offering him the closed umbrella, practically forcing it in his hand. He didn't know what to say as he held the umbrella, and watched her turn, a smile stretched across her face. She returned the way she'd come, her umbrella clearing a cylinder of space around her.

It was so strange, as if she'd read his mind, but of course she'd seen him getting wet. Jergenson thought about the time he had seen a stranger walking through his neighborhood during a rainstorm. What did he do? He called the cops – that's what he did. Jergenson opened the umbrella and looked it over. He never thought he'd be so appreciative of something so common. He would need to look for a drier spot, somewhere with more cover. He figured it was going to be a long, uncomfortable night. He looked up, wanting to say thank you to the lady, but she had already gone inside.

He followed the avenue for half an hour in a direction he felt was right, passing convenient stores excessively lit in brilliant white and small temples with rows of red lamps flanking statues of mysterious gods. He could see inside some of the homes with their doors opened to let in the air. There were children studying, mothers cooking and fathers watching TV just like anywhere and he wondered why he hadn't noticed that before.

Then, just as he passed between the cover of two buildings, holding the umbrella like his life depended on it, a man stepped out from what looked like a small bar. Jergenson was forced to stop on the slippery pavement to avoid hitting him. The man's eyes grew wide.

"Welcome!" He smiled and waved Jergenson in. Jergenson could see there were three people already inside. A bartender, a waitress and one other patron sitting at a four-stool bar. Above this was a TV with a local baseball game playing. Ah, he realized, the man was a baseball fan and knew him from his Taiwanese team. "Welcome – welcome!" The man waved, obviously insisting that Jergenson join them. Glancing up into the darkness of night ahead of him, the invitation to spend some time out of the rain was a small relief, so he went in.

Yes, he tried to tell them he had no money. He patted and pulled out his pockets. But those people in there were so impressed at having a famous baseball star in their little bar, they bought him drinks. "Welcome!" The man slapped his back and tapped his beer bottle with Jergenson's before taking a swig. It was clear no one in the bar knew much English and the few words they did know were repeated often. Over the next few hours they used a lot of sign language and gestures like they were playing a game of Charades. They watched the baseball game and the man showed Jergenson the way he batted and Jergenson showed him his way. They drew words on napkins to try to explain things and looked over a few baseball magazines the bartender kept on a stand across from the bar and they finished a number of bottles that collected on the counter like bowling pins and Jergenson forgot all about being lost.

Jergenson didn't know when he had gone to

sleep, but he woke up on the couch besides the magazine rack. A thin wool blanket covered him. The room was empty. The lights were off, but it wasn't dark, sunlight leaked in around the front door. A clock above the bar showed it was late morning. He got up, found the restroom, washed his face and then stumbled out into the daylight. As he waited for his eyes to adjust, a man called out to him from across the street. It was the stranger he had drunk with all night. His biggest fan, he was sure. The man worked in a scooter repair shop, and had a greasy rag in one hand, a screwdriver in the other. The stranger waved him over and called out to someone deeper inside the shop. Jergenson waved back and crossed the avenue. As he neared the garage, a girl of no more than twelve came out of a back room. She introduced herself in fairly good English, saying the man was her father. Well, when Jergenson heard her speak English, he felt like he had found his way out of a long cave. In a blur of words he explained to her that he didn't have any money, but needed to get back to Taipei. He said he would gladly pay for all the expenses.

They did give him a ride home. The man and his daughter seemed proud to have the baseball star with them the way they kept smiling and showing him things that the locals were proud of, even took him to lunch before heading off. He felt like some sort of royalty as they got on the highway in the old van the man owned. Hours later, when they arrived outside his high-rise apartment, he told the girl to wait so he could get some money. When she translated this to her father, he became adamant about not wanting payment. Over and over Jergenson told the girl he would pay them, but her father would not agree. Seeing the man push back so much made Jergenson give up on trying to reimburse him for the ride. As he stood beside the van, he asked the girl if they wanted his autograph. It was the least he could do for such a big fan. She and her father talked for a time, and it almost appeared as if they were avoiding him because they didn't understand what he was saying. "An autograph," he said, "From a baseball player. It's what we do in America." The father said something and the girl translated: "We don't need anything." The man seemed ready to leave, and Jergenson could understand why. They had a two-hour drive back to their home. Then the girl said something that left him speechless, and unable to do anything but stand there and watch them drive away. And then he stood there a while longer.

    You already know where he ended up. I don't need to say anything about that. He started playing a little different after that. Trusted his teammates, listened to the coach, didn't always try to hit the fence. He found he was pretty good at moving the bases up, getting singles, sometimes doubles. He started writing cards to his wife. Didn't even know if she'd reply, but he wrote her every week. His stats shot up. Eight months later, an American scout, sitting in those noisy Taiwanese stands, wrote up a good report on him, saying he was batting like a superstar. Two American teams made him an offer to return to the States. It was hard leaving. His Taiwanese teammates and coach had become his best friends.

What's that? What did the girl say to him? She told him, with that bluntness children often have, that they had no idea that he played baseball. You see, they didn't know he was a big league player. They weren't fans. And that truly was a curveball for him. To them he was just a stranger.

About the Author

Patrick Wayland was born during a hurricane in Corpus Christi, Texas. He graduated from The University of Texas at San Antonio, worked in Silicon Valley in the high-tech industry and later studied Asian languages in Hong Kong and Taiwan. Author of *The Jade Lady*, Patrick lives in Taipei and spends his time walking the line between technology and culture. Visit him at patrickwayland.wordpress.com.

Gap Years

by
Tony Messina
(contains adult language)

She orders fried chicken bits, a log of tofu,
some cauliflower, and a pile of breaded squid. We
watch as the combination is diced, deep-fried,
tossed with sautéed garlic and chili peppers and
slid into a paper bag through a wide-mouthed
funnel.

"Do you want anything else?" Steph asks me
as we grab our food.

Are you kidding?

More. We need more.

At home only two plastic containers of milk
tea and a half-eaten scallion pancake live on

amongst a scattering of grease-stained wrappers and plastic bags that roll like tumbleweeds in the full blast of the air conditioner.

"Do you want to watch TV?" I ask.

"Sure. You can if you want," she says, not looking up from her phone. The soft flesh just below my waist spasms painfully, a signal of desperation from my organs. But the last thing I want to do is stand up.

Last weekend it was two hours of shouting followed by Domino's delivery. A night or two before that I actually punched a hole in the sheetrock. One bandage and several apologies later found Steph and I at Coldstone, putting away at least a full pint each. Other people have make-up sex, we consume.

Neither of us has to go to work tomorrow and I decide an impromptu trip to the beach is just what we need. But Steph is set on staying home and finishing the revision of a paper she promised her professor weeks ago. Also, I need a haircut, the apartment is a mess, and I haven't been running in days. Keeping a full, balanced, schedule without any large blocks of free time is imperative if I don't want to go back on the meds. So is a healthy diet and consistent exercise.

The curtains hang open just enough for a crack of sunlight to wedge onto the slat of hardwood floor between my feet. This is the first day it hasn't rained all week. It's a Thursday, we probably would have had the entire beach to ourselves.

Steph notices me rubbing my knuckles, the largest of which is still pink and slightly swollen. Her eyes shrink and her forehead grows. Her sad face. I try not to make eye contact. There's just no room in our lives for impromptu anymore, and I've given up looking for someone to blame.

* * *

Fridays are our early days. Steph and I both teach evenings but at opposite ends of the city. We walk to the MRT together and our trains arrive at the same time, as usual. She likes to stand near the door of her train and wave at me, across the platform, through the door of mine. As I begin to wave, a skinny college student with jean shorts riding up her ass strolls down the platform between us. The movement of the train immediately relocates my field of vision from the shadowed smile of her exposed cheeks to the darkness of the tunnel. It's not until I've found a seat and begun reading that I realize it's possible Steph saw me, likely she was waving right at me when I ogled that girl. And I try to remember what it's like to care about things like that.

I fast-walk the eight minutes from my station to the school and clock in at exactly two o'clock. The first four classes go off without me losing my temper a single time and my teaching assistant doesn't try to hide her relief.

"You're in a good mood today!" she says.

"Am I usually not?" I ask.

"Umm. Maybe no," she says.

The last class of the night is a one-hour private lesson with Tina, a Taiwanese businesswoman one year my senior. Thirty minutes of grammar review takes its toll on both of us. She asks if we can just have conversation practice for the rest of the lesson.

"How much longer will you stay in Taiwan?" she asks.

"One more year. I'm applying for graduate school now and I'll be leaving in about a year," I say.

The conversation goes on and I'm perched somewhere on the ceiling, looking down, hearing myself say the same things I've said to every new person I've met in the past four months. "International relations, No, I haven't studied much Chinese these past two years, but I'm studying hard now, It would, after all, help a lot for this degree, *Dui bu qi,* but we can't speak Chinese now, you know Scott would kill us."

And I hear her laugh and laugh.

What I don't hear is the other part of my usual response, the part where I say something like, "Oh, my girlfriend is getting her Ph.D. here in Taipei now, but will be able to transfer to a school in the States next year. We're applying for schools in the same cities. We're going to go together."

We've already gone ten minutes past the end

of class when I ask if she has any last questions about today's lesson.

She suddenly looks away, cheeks flush with blood, and asks, "Do you have a girlfriend?"

It's at least a full minute before I respond and by then the salty odor of the sea has already overwhelmed me.

* * *

Steph and I play chess. She makes a point of not getting annoyed when I take so long because she is just as slow. Or maybe it's just because she knows I'm so sensitive about it. Chess has never been my strong suit, and while it's possible that this is because I only play it intermittently, sometimes going years between games, I think my demeanor is just as much to blame. It's too easily that I become excited, attack relentlessly at the first sign of weakness, and run right into a trap. Just as often I'll simply miss the obvious outright, losing my queen in a moment of carelessness. I've decided our next game will not go this way.

Before each move I methodically examine every possible path for both her pieces and mine, plot steps two, three, four turns in advance. Forty-five minutes into our first match, we appear to be at a stalemate, each having lost only some pawns. However, I control most of the center of the board and know it's only a matter of time before my winning move materializes. On my next turn I continue with the strategy, see that her knight can take my bishop if I'm not careful, that my queen is the only thing preventing her rook from advancing and as such shouldn't be moved, and that it is my front most bishop and knight that I should use to mount the next offensive. But I see something else as well. If I make the move I planned, then in the next turn she'll humor me, pretend she doesn't see the obvious and move somewhere else, setting her trap. The turn after that the next pieces of her net will fall into place and by then it will be too late. In four turns, we'll be together in the US, attending grad school and never having time for weekend dinner parties or spontaneous trips to the coast. Two moves later and it's shared bank accounts, my life's savings going toward her student loans. White rook to F7 and it's a kid, a little boy, and a night job for me to help support them both. White pawn to G5 and it's her mother moving halfway across the world to permanently take over our guest bedroom. Five, six, seven, moves from now and it's just my future, shrinking, shrinking, shrinking. White Queen to E3. Checkmate. I flip over the board, run in the bathroom and lock the door, knowing that explaining myself would be pointless. I had agreed to play. Losing was always an option.

* * *

I only teach three classes on Saturday, but they are spaced in a way to require me to be at the school all day. Afterwards, Steph and I each refuse invitations to go out drinking so that we can wake up early on Sunday, bike a few kilometers, then spend the rest of the day studying in a coffee shop. There is nothing worth watching on any of the English language channels, so we tune to an episode of a series we've already seen to serve as background noise. This, I know, is risky behavior. The less preoccupied we are, the more likely we'll speak to one another.

She pushes aside the last portion of a *shuei jian bao*, the transparent noodles and gnarled pork ball protruding from the half eaten dough at jagged angles, and turns to me as I silently curse my mistake.

"Have you signed up for the GRE yet?" she asks.

"Not yet," I tell her.

"We don't have that much time, you know," she says.

"I know," I whisper.

"I can't hear you," she says.

"Just, stop putting so much pressure on me," I say.

The first year we lived together I'd leave the apartment anytime an incipient argument threatened to mature. There's a city park nearby and one or two laps around it were usually enough to settle me down. The problem was, these little walks had the opposite effect on Steph. If I left her alone when things between us weren't perfectly stable, her fear and rage would spread like a virus. She'd call me a few minutes into each walk, alternating between tears, accusations, and feral yells. These were the times I wanted to hurt her the most, but of course I never could.

* * *

The next week brings Steph's final exams, leaving me to commute to work on my own. On the way to the MRT I pass a local college campus. Some students outside flock to me, the *wai guo ren,* with some sort of survey to fill out. The questions are all pretty much what I'd expected, things about my thoughts on the country, its culture, what I had wished to accomplish when I first moved here and if I had currently made any progress on doing so. The leader of the three wears a polo shirt completely unbuttoned. While she speaks to one of the other girls in Chinese, I glance at her taut breasts and get a mental image of Steph about 15 pounds ago, before books and television dominated our lives.

* * *

It was on one of those nights in the park that a stray dog emerges from the blackness of the empty amphitheater and climbs down my throat.

* * *

The next time I have class with Tina I know it will be our last. She shows up late, wearing a miniskirt and sequined sleeveless top. I ask if she has plans after class. When she says no I ask if she has just come from work and she shakes her head.

We were meant to review a correspondence she wrote to a client, but she's forgotten to bring it. I ask if she'd like to do a writing exercise now, to make up for it, but she remains impermeable. Our staring contest ends when, in resignation, I walk up to the board and give a five-minute presentation on the past perfect versus the past simple.

"Your girlfriend's English must be very good," she says.

"It is," I say after a moment's hesitation. "She's studying English literature at *Tai Da*".

"Wow," she says, clapping a single time. "So her English is much better than mine?"

I look at the clock. There's still half an hour of this to survive. "I don't know," I say. "I don't think it's good to compare"

"Don't you?"

* * *

The next time Steph asks me about the GRE I explode into tears. Eventually, she registers for the test for me and we go out to my favorite local place for some *nio pai*, Taiwanese steak and noodles.

After the meal we're both so happy we walk

all the way from the night market to the movie theatre, like we used to, holding hands the entire way. At home we make love and she helps me do a web search for English-speaking therapists in Taipei. There are only two and both charge around one hundred US dollars an hour. Completely unmanageable on our budget. Our solution is to spend two hours composing detailed schedules for ourselves, schedules which will allot even more time for study and exercise.

The first round of college applications has approached us, so the occasional weekend hiking trip or concert has ceased completely. And it's ok. Really, ok. Because this is our future, this is us, challenging ourselves, refusing to settle for the what could be a comfortable life in Taiwan and that's laudable. Occasionally I'll run a question by Steph and she offers nothing but assistance. This is what we want. This is how we get it.

Two weeks pass and I've been sleeping roughly 4 hours a night. At best. The applications are no longer as simple. Male: *check*. Term applying for: *Fall 2014*. Statement of purpose: ...?. I am caught in some strange parallel of the world I've come from and the world I'm going back to. And I know they are no longer the same place. Things change. Social trends are fickle; languages, evolutionary. People call me unstable, but really it's the world that's volatile. Steph sees the changes in me and urges me to go to bed before twelve.

The next morning it's Tina I wake up next to,

Tina looking into my eyes saying good morning in her sleepy voice, Tina making the coffee while I cut the guava and rose apples and Tina sucking my cock while we're both supposed to be getting ready for work. And for some reason, this makes sense.

I go to school and teach children, tell them how to say things in English while periodically signaling for them to throw a sticky ball at the whiteboard. They laugh and the words coming out of my mouth might not even be English anymore, but it's ok. It's ok because they laugh so I keep talking and when I get home, it's Steph again. Steph and me. Us. We watch TV together. We talk about our respective days and we put on the Jack Johnson album and make love and I wonder if maybe one day she'll let me drizzle chocolate syrup over her nipples or feed her strawberries in the bathtub we don't have or rest a Big Mac on her bare ass so I can gobble it up without using my hands.

* * *

With a massive typhoon impending, the government has already closed school for tomorrow. Steph's called to tell me she'll stop by the supermarket after work to get supplies. That leaves me about an hour and a half of alone time, enough for at least two laps around the park. On the first straightaway the pre-typhoon skies erupt. The wind pushes the water in streaks down my glasses and eventually right into my eyes. My windbreaker, T-

Shirt, shorts, sneakers, and socks are completely soaked through.

The rain stops in time for my post-jog walk, but does little to dry me off. A man seated under a canopy in front of a closed coffee shop stands abruptly upon my approach.

His feet make sloppy slaps against the wet pavement as he tries to catch up with me, but I keep my pace.

"Hallo. Hallo. Ex-cuse me," he yells. This man is so happy there's no question he's mentally unwell.

It's not the first time I've been approached by a homeless person who just wants to talk to a foreigner and undoubtedly get some money off him. But I'm too exhausted to follow my usual plan of walking down well-lit streets until he gets bored and trails off. We stop at the door of my apartment building. He stands in wait, as if he were an honored guest while I fumble with my keys.

"You here how long?" he asks.

The keys fall to the ground and I drop to retrieve them before he can. "I'm an English teacher," I say, knowing it doesn't really answer his questions but think that it's ok as long as I say something. Everything will be alright as long it's me, my voice, making the words over and over again.

"Oh, so good, so good. Student?" he asks, pointing in the direction of the local university. "You study Chinese?"

"A little," I say. "I'm a teacher, but I do study some Chinese. *Yi dian dian*".

He claps and squeals as if I've just performed a magic trick. "You Chinese so good. You here how long?"

Behind him, Steph lumbers under the awning of the shops, two full bags in her arms. Seeing her try so desperately to avoid stepping into any puddles makes me feel like a child watching another child play a game I've outgrown.

"You go back America?" he asks, oblivious to my distraction.

"I'm going to go…." I start, before Steph notices me. Her eyes widen, her nostrils narrow, and she exhales a groan that I cannot hear. Her angry face. She probably assumes I've again made the mistake of humoring an old, crazy man. Of wasting everyone's precious time with my naivety. And suddenly, I'm hungry. Fucking starved.

I run. Take off toward the nearest night market. Everything in my body pushes my fat-ass forward, legs churning harder than ever before. I don't look back, swerve between people, almost cause a bicycler to tumble and swear that for at least two full minutes my feet never once strike the ground. In an instant it becomes clear to me that the goal is to stretch out my stride and have my legs propel me to the moon. When I was a kid, my grandfather actually convinced me it was made of cheese. Tonight I'm going to cum all over it. Smash it to bits with my dick, then eat it. I want to look back, find the hobo and take him with me, but it's impossible. Find Tina and have her teach me what it feels like to fuck her before I fly away into orbit forever.

I can't stop moving.

After I've reached the first tenuous alley of the marketplace, the downpour begins again.

It's at least an hour before she finds me, seated, legs sprawled in a mass of water. Most of the vendors have packed up early because of the storm. Choosing to forego our usual fencing match of accusations and explanations, thrusts and ripostes, she instead pulls me up and wraps her arms around me.

"I was so worried," she whispers, but really, all I can focus on is the fragrance wafting up from the plastic grocery bag still hanging off her wrist.

She leads me to a cab and tells the driver our address in Chinese. I had no idea I'd run so far from home. The bag rustles as she digs through it with both hands.

"I know our anniversary isn't until Tuesday, but I want you to have this now. I made it," she says, handing me a picture frame.

Two photos rest atop each other at an uneven angle, both of them of us. On top, the two of us in front of our apartment building the day we moved in. Underneath, us at a restaurant last weekend. I don't even remember the second one being taken. The photos are propped on a piece of card where a hand-drawn design vines between the photos and a mathematical formula written in bubble letters: "1+1=2."

"We can do it, baby," she says laying her arm across my lap.

And I know that really, down the highway somewhere, I'm still running, cruising along at light speed and she'll never be able to catch me.

About the Author

Tony Messina spent the past three years in Taipei, Taiwan, teaching English, studying Mandarin, writing, and eating. He is currently an MFA in Creative Writing candidate (fiction) at the University of Notre Dame (2015).

Superstition

by
Amanda Miao

The next two flights of stairs loom ahead, and Jia-ying slumps down on one of the steps. Tears she managed to control the first six floors begin to trickle down her cheeks. With a resolution she hasn't known she possessed, she pulls herself to her feet and continues to slowly make her way to the eighth floor.

Home has never seemed so far away, she thinks limping with a bloody leg and a torn uniform skirt. Her thoughts are on the coin fortune-telling and the fact that all this bad luck started after playing that stupid game.

Finally, she reaches the large metal door and rings the doorbell, too hurt to try to dig her keys out of her schoolbag. The door opens, revealing her mother's pinched face, eyebrows drawn in anger.

"Jia-ying, the school called and said- What happened to your leg!" her mom cries, dropping the cordless phone as she stares at her daughter's disheveled appearance.

Already having passed the breaking point at the sixth floor, Jia-ying's tears start to pour in earnest as she decides to confess everything in hopes that her mother will help her find a way to end her bad luck.

* * *

Apples, oranges, and instant noodles were carefully arranged around a small bowl filled with incense ashes on a fold-up table. Jia-ying stared with longing at the food, tugging impatiently at the ends of her long black hair before crossing her arms. No one was allowed to eat before the offerings were given and the ghost money was burnt. A bunch of superstitious nonsense. All of ghost month was.

Eyeing the large red apples, Jia-ying glanced down the mostly empty sidewalk and back towards the apartment complex's door. Her mother and father had just run back up to get the rest of the ghost money, her obnoxious little brother in tow. He got excited about every holiday and custom no matter how ridiculous it was.

No one in sight, she quickly snatched an apple off the table and took a bite, chewing quickly.

"Sister!" a whiny voice yelled.

Jia-ying jumped in surprise, trading guilt for anger as she whipped around to find her little brother with a pout on his round face. "Watch it, dummy! You practically scared me to death!"

"Sister, you are not supposed to talk about death during ghost month!" he scolded, shaking his pudgy finger at her. "And you can't eat before the offerings! Mama's gonna get mad. Apples mean peace and you are stealing the ghosts' peace!"

"Oh, shut up. Mama won't be mad if she doesn't know, and only six-year olds and old people believe in ghosts," Jia-ying told him, taking another defiant bite of the apple. "When you are in high school, you won't believe in them either."

They both turned, argument temporarily forgotten, when they heard footsteps coming towards them. Jia-ying dropped the apple into her large purse, and glared at her brother, "Don't you dare tell Mama or you're done for, got it?"

His response was to stick his tongue out at her, but she knew he wouldn't tell. Whiny or not, he still looked up to his big sister.

"Jia-ying! Ah Jie! Come help your mother carry these bags!" their father called, hefting two of his own bags filled with gold and red paper. Jumping with excitement, her little brother grabbed a bag and took it over to the small metal brazier.

"Jia-ying," her mother said, dark brown eyes glaring at her daughter. "Come over here and help. We have a lot of ghost money to burn. Don't you want your father's bookstore to do well?"

Rolling her eyes, Jia-ying gave a put-upon sigh. "Mom, it's 32 degrees out here. I'm in shorts and a tank top and I'm still dying of the heat. Now you want to make me stand next to an open flame?"

"Jia-ying!" her mother snapped, as she set down the bag of money with a thud, "Don't talk about dying during ghost month. And as you can see, your father, brother, and I are all in the same boat and you don't hear us complaining, do you?"

"Can't I just light the incense and go? I'm meeting some friends for lunch and I don't want my clothes to have that burnt-paper smell," Jia-ying said, smoothing her wrinkled tank top.

"Fine, I don't want the ghost to get offended by your bad attitude anyway. Come on, Ah Jie, you want to light the incense sticks too?" her mother asked, smiling when her son practically jumped up and down while nodding his head.

To Jia-ying's annoyance, it took far too long to light the incense sticks and bow, but as soon as her family placed the sticks in the incense ashes, she was off running to the bus stop. Her mom called back after her, reminding her not to stay out late and a million other warnings that Jia-ying had heard over and over. With a backwards wave, she continued running, shoving her headphones over her ears and turning up her iPod, glad to finally be free.

* * *

"You ate an offering before prayers were said?" her mother asks with disapproval. Jia-ying nods sadly from where she is sitting on the couch, sipping green tea.

"I admit your attitude leaves a lot to be desired," her mother starts, smoothing back her dark black hair behind her ear. She stops her scolding when she sees tears gather in Jia-ying's eyes again. With a sigh, her mother asks, "Is that all?"

Jia-ying bites her lip. She wishes that were her only offense...

* * *

"Aiyo, it's started," Jia-ying complained to her best friend.

"What's started?" Momo asked after she pinned back her short black tresses.

Crossing her arms atop her desk and laying her head on top of them, Jia-ying looked up. "All the ghost talk. 'Don't whistle at night, you'll call the ghosts!' 'Don't look over your shoulder, the ghost will weaken you that way!' 'Don't say die!'" she mimicked in her mom's sternest voice.

Momo stopped fiddling with her hairpins, and leaned over her desk, her eyes wide as she said in a horrified whisper, "You say die during ghost month?"

"Oh, Momo! Not you too!" Jia-ying

exclaimed, making the younger girl jump. "You know it's all just superstition. Right?"

Shifting her eyes away from Jia-ying and towards the large windows of their classroom, Momo gave a little shrug, "Oh, yeah, of course. It's just..." She looked away from all the uniformed students outside carrying books and hurrying to classes.

"I mean, wouldn't it be a good idea to just be careful this month? After all, last night on the news you heard about the girl who drowned..." Momo's voice trailed off in concern, glancing nervously around, as if the ghosts were eavesdropping that very minute.

Jia-ying rolled her eyes, "People drown all the time. The news only gets excited about it during ghost month because the ghosts in the water are *supposed* to be stronger now."

"But the news also said more people drown in ghost month than any other time of the year," her friend said uncertainly, twirling her pencil in her hands.

"Well, it's summer, and lucky kids who don't have to go to summer school are, of course, going to go to the beach. More people at the beach, more chances to drown. See? Simple mathematics. Nothing to do with ghosts." Jia-ying sat back in her seat with a self-satisfied grin, smoothing her skirts with a confident flick of her hand. Her friend seemed less sure about this explanation, but nodded her head reluctantly anyway. Probably in an effort to avoid talking more about the ghosts. Many people got jumpy like that during the lunar month of July, Jia-ying thought with an inward sigh.

"Hey, ladies!" a loud masculine voice said, dropping his hands on Jia-ying's shoulders as she and Momo squealed in surprise.

"Guo-he!" Jia-ying yelled in a high-pitched voice, turning to slap the taller boy on the arm. Nearby classmates laughed and joked while she continued to smack him and he pretended that it hurt.

Dodging the last playful blow, Guo-he took a seat in the desk next to her, "What's this I hear? Jiajia's not afraid of ghosts?" He raised his eyebrows in mock surprise, then made a tsking sound when she nodded.

"Well, if you're not afraid, then how about we do some coin fortune-telling?" he challenged, his black eyes alight with mischief.

"Jiajia," Momo hissed, tugging on her friend's sleeve. Jia-ying gave Guo-he a grin filled with challenge. It was the look that always preempted trouble, usually of Jia-ying's making. Momo cast a glare in Guo-he's direction and shook her head, but the two ignored her, locked in their own competitive battle.

"Fine. I'm not scared. Who's got a piece of paper?" Jia-ying asked, taking out a pen and a ten-dollar coin.

A smile lit up Guo-he's face as he reached across and stole a paper from his friend's schoolbag as his friend squawked in protest. They quickly filled the paper out with numbers and the Chinese characters for *yes* and *no*. Then Guo-he pretended to call on the ghosts for their advice in a voice that wavered in a mocking impression of the temple fortune-tellers' voices, while Jia-ying giggled the whole time.

A strong wind blew suddenly in through the open front door, sending the other girls in class shrieking as they scrambled to grab skirts or papers flying around the cramped classroom.

Momo's face paled as she looked from the sunlit door to her friends, "Guys, are you sure you wanna do this?"

"Oh, Momo," Jia-ying laughed, pinching her friend's cheek.

"Alright!" Guo-he said, tapping the piece of paper and bringing Jia-ying's attention back to him. "Now, Jiajia, call on the ghosts to answer your question, and then ask away."

Holding the coin, Jia-ying asked for the ghost's help, trying to keep back her giggles as Guo-he folded his hands prayer-like and bowed his head. "This question's for you, Momo," she teased, smiling broadly at her friend's scowling face. "Are ghosts real?"

Jia-ying put the coin down on the middle of the paper, glanced at where the *no* was and closed her eyes, as if communing with the spirits. Pretending to chant, Jia-ying slid the coin in the direction of *no* slowly, pretending she was fighting with a ghostly hand.

Silence fell from the students that had gathered around nearby to watch, and Jia-ying opened her eyes, laughing. "Oh, come on, you don't..." Her voice trailed off as she stared down at the paper. The silver coin rested on top of the character for *yes*.

Momo's eyes were wide, "Jiajia..."

Even Guo-he looked a bit subdued. "It seemed to just jump from your finger..."

"Oh, come on," Jia-ying said, forcing some playfulness into her voice. "I'll just do it again and you can see the real answer."

"No, come on, Jiajia," Momo pleaded, "Just thank the ghost for its help and ask it to leave. You have to ask it to leave or —"

"Everyone, sit down!" a voice yelled from the doorway. Teacher Li, a short woman with thick glasses and a severe bob cut, glowered from the front of the classroom. All talking stopped instantly as students scrambled to their desks, not wishing to anger the strict math instructor.

Jia-ying crumpled up the fortune-telling paper. She dropped the coin in her pocket before turning to face forward.

"Your math exams from last week," she said with a disapproval as she gave the tests to another student to hand back. "All students with less than fifty percent will receive five hits with the ruler! I'm very disappointed in you! Summer school is not a time for play! If you want to get into a good university..."

Jia-ying tuned out the rest of Teacher Li's lecture, and reached for her paper. Yelping in a surprise at the sting of pain, she stuck her index finger in her mouth, trying to stop the paper-cut from bleeding.

"Did you thank the ghost and ask it to leave?" Momo hissed, staring with worry at her friend's injured finger.

"Classmate Jia-ying!" Teacher Li snapped.

Taking her finger out of her mouth quickly, Jia-ying's eyes snapped to the front, "Yes, Teacher Li?"

"I believe you scored low on this exam as well," her teacher said with disappointment, pointing to the line of students that had formed in the front of the classroom, the first boy already holding out his hand, palm up.

It was impossible. Jia-ying was very good at math, her exams were always high scores... But when she glanced down at her paper, she saw a large red 45% drawn and circled. With a sickening feeling, she stood up and walked towards the end of the line, her face burning a deep red.

How could this have happened? she thought while biting her lip. Then a worse thought popped into her head, *what would her mother do when she found out about the low score?*

It had been hours ago, but Jia-ying's hand still stung from the five hits she'd received in math class. Pulling on her white uniform shirt again, she stared at the large black stain she had gotten at the calligraphy club. The brush had almost seemed to jump out of her hand, ink flying in every direction.

She sighed, kicking rocks on the sidewalk in frustration as she headed to the bus station. One of the rocks flew up higher than she intended, hitting some poor woman in the back of her leg. Bowing repeatedly, Jia-ying apologized as she picked up her pace and ran to the bus stop.

Taking out her cell-phone yet again to complain to Momo about the bad day's catastrophes, she hit the unlock key only to have a heavyset man running to the bus slam into her, sending the phone flying from her hands. The pink sticker-covered phone landed with an ominous crack in the road just in time to be run over by one of the many buses arriving at the bus stop.

Staring in horror at the remaining pieces of her cell phone that littered the street, Jia-ying looked up too late to see her bus pulling away from the curb.

"Wait!" she yelled, running after the bus, knowing the next one wouldn't be along for twenty minutes, and would undoubtedly be crowded. With a puff of dark exhaust, the bus sped off, leaving Jia-ying on the sidewalk, coughing and shaking her fist.

There was no place to sit on the benches at the stop, so she paced, worrying at her ruined blouse and the growing list of bad news she would have to tell her mother. Eventually, the next bus came, but was so crowded no other passengers were allowed on. Another wait ensued, as the sky clouded over and fat drops of rain began to fall.

Searching her bag, Jia-ying discovered she hadn't brought her umbrella and held her schoolbag over her head, moaning about her horrible luck. A tiny niggling thought kept trying to intrude. An eerie voice in her head that hinted maybe, just maybe, her mom wasn't completely wrong. If, and a big if, ghosts were real, she'd definitely done a lot to tick them off.

The next bus arrived and pushed those thoughts away as she tried to cram herself in with the other passengers. She managed to get hit by the automatic door for her troubles, but at least she was on, even if she was squashed up against the large bus windows.

It took twice as long to get home now that the after-work traffic was in full swing, and it was dark by the time she paid for the bus and stepped off. Her mind, deep in misery that seemed to grow heavier as she neared home, made her forget to check when stepping off the bus, and she glanced right just before the bicyclist slammed into her.

* * *

Her mother's face pales as she listens to Jia-ying's story. "Jia-ying-a, how could you do that? You know, I just heard on the news of a girl who played the fortune-telling game and was hit by a car! Come on, let me fix your leg and we are going straight to the temple. You need to tell the priest what happened and ask for his help to get the ghost to go away. Thank goodness your father took your brother to his Taekwondo practice today."

With the efficiency her mother is famous for, she has Jia-ying fixed up in no time. She gives her daughter a piece of lucky red paper with symbols of protection for added security before they hop on the scooter and head down to the local temple.

Jia-ying has never before been so glad to see the colorful carved pillars of the temple and the ornate roof that houses the carefully-carved statues of the various land gods and gods of luck that the temple is famous for. Incense hangs heavily throughout the spread-out temple, floating hazily until escaping into the dark and carrying the prayers of worshippers into the sky and to the surrounding lands.

A priest in simple yellow and red robes greets them, and her mother wastes no time in explaining her daughter's trouble. The temple priest shakes his head and listens solemnly, before looking at Jia-ying with a sigh.

"Come, I will throw the fortune sticks, consult my charts, and see how we can help your daughter." They follow the priest off to the left of the large bowl holding a large amount of ashes and numerous incense sticks. A sparsely furnished office is filled with papers, charts, lucky red and white paper, and instruments for fortune-telling line bookshelves in three of the walls and surround a long wooden table.

The priest gestures for them to take a seat at the table before pulling out a chart and a small bamboo cylinder filled with flat wooden sticks. The necessary information of Jia-ying's birthday, both in the western and lunar calendar, her blood type, along with other pertinent facts are given.

Jia-ying watches nervously as he consults the charts, often saying 'hhmm' with concern.

He looks up from the charts, "Do you still have the coin from the fortune-telling game?"

Nodding, Jia-ying produces the coin and makes to hand it to the priest, but he just tells her to set it on the table. For a few moments, he gazes at it adding a few more 'hhmms'.

"Alright, pick up the coin and come with me to the main temple," he says, grabbing the bamboo cylinder filled with wooden sticks. Jia-ying and her mother scramble to do as instructed and follow him back into the cavernous part of the temple that houses colorful statues of the gods lining the back wall. Gifts of food crowd tables in front of them, as well as more bowls of ashes and incense sticks.

"Now, stand in front here, hold the coin and shake this bamboo cup until I say," the priest instructs, handing it to her. Taking her place, she accepts the bamboo cup with shaking hands, doing as she is told. Eventually three sticks stand out above the others. The priest grabs those and makes a few more 'hmmms' while nodding.

Nerves stretched taught and feeling a little lightheaded from the thick concentration of incense, Jia-ying is ready to pass out when the priest finally speaks again.

"Come, back to the office. I know what we can do to help your daughter," he says with a wave of his hand, leading them back. Mother and daughter follow anxiously.

Back in the office, the priest explains that the ghost is a particularly stubborn one and is quite angered by Jia-ying's disrespect. Both the priest and her mother stare at her with a shake of their heads. It's difficult, but she manages not to flush under the intense disapproval.

"What can I do to make it right?" she pleads, just wanting to go back home and leave this nightmare behind her.

"Well, for one, you can apologize to the ghost. Ask for forgiveness. That should help, however, the ghost is tied to this coin. You must put this coin in a mix of water and ashes from some lucky paper I will give you. Leave it in the mixture for the rest of the ghost month and then the coin will be cleansed and you can get rid of it without fear," he explains.

Jia-ying sighs in relief, but he continues, "However! You must not let anyone else touch this coin or the ghost will haunt that person instead, understand?" Both mother and daughter nod their heads fervently, thanking the priest over and over.

Before they leave, he gives them more lucky paper and repeats the instructions while Jia-ying's mother makes a donation to the temple. In no time they are back home, the apartment still silent and empty.

"Let's make this mixture before your father and brother come home," her mother says. She lays out a tablecloth on the table, and Jia-ying puts the coin down carefully on top. They head to the back balcony to burn the lucky paper in a small metal bucket.

While they watch the paper burn, they suddenly become aware of soft padding footsteps making their way through the kitchen and to the balcony.

"Mama," Jia-ying hears her brother's voice call.

Her mother's head snaps up and towards the screen door, "Ah Jie! You're home!"

"Yeah, father dropped me off before going to get dinner. What are you guys doing? And what was this coin doing on the table?" he asks, holding up the silver coin.

Jia-ying looks at her mother, eyes wide-open in horror, just as her mother lets out a strangled cry

Ah Jie stares at them in confusion. "What?"

And maybe it is the stress of the horrible day, or the finding out that ghosts are real and not all that friendly and possibly now after her brother, but Jia-ying swears she can hear an eerie chuckle on the wind; a creaky voice telling her not to worry, it's someone else's problem now.

About the Author

Amanda Miao spent eight years in Taiwan as an English teacher. Now her writing desk is situated in southern California where she writes on subjects more academic than fantasy (she hopes) as she works toward a Master's degree in Linguistics. Someday she hopes to visit Taiwan (her home away from home), and get back to writing about the worlds and characters taking up space in her head.

The Collector

by
J. J. Green

The man browsed the items for sale, taking
things from the shelves and glancing at them before
pushing them back onto a different shelf. He wasn't
really looking at them, Chiang noted. Computer
keyboards, credit cards, kitchen utensils, ornaments.
Flotsam and jetsam of the pre-Peak Heat world
filled Chiang's shop, and the man seemed to be
interested in all and none of it. He drifted over to a
stack of photographs, and thumbed through them.
He took a handful to the shop front. Holding the
images up to the window, he peered at them in the
strong beams of sunlight. Chiang caught every
glance the man shot in his direction, and responded

with a glare.

"How much do you want for this?"

Chiang jumped. A young woman stood in front of him, waving a photograph in his face. It was a wide view of Shida night market, taken in the first half of the twenty-first century as far as Chiang could tell, probably more than fifty years ago. The night markets had changed little over the five decades spanning the end of the twentieth century and the beginning of the twenty-first.

"What can you give me for it? Preserved food? Good quality? Or something fresh?"

The woman's brows knit. "I was hoping you accepted money."

Chiang's eyes drifted to the man as he was ambling towards the large, open messages book that rested on a podium at the back of the shop.

"Not many businesses accepting money yet. What if I take it but can't use it?" he said.

"But I have thousands of dollars. My wages."

"Government job, eh?" He shook his head and sighed.

The woman looked down. "It was the only work I could get."

Chiang took the photograph from her. It was one of the first he had collected, scrabbling in the ruins of abandoned buildings when global temperatures had finally started to fall, and life was no longer a desperate, day-to-day survival. "Is there a reason you want this one in particular?"

"My father told me once my grandfather

worked at Shida market. He had a beef noodle stand. The best in the market. The queue went round the block. Until the police turned up of course." She smiled.

"Really? What else did your father tell you?"

"Oh, so many things..."

At the back of the shop the man was leafing through the messages book, scanning each page. Chiang sat down on the tall stool behind his shop counter and folded his arms.

"... In the evenings the streets were so full - people could hardly walk. "Everything was sold there. Everything. Live chickens the stallholders would kill and pluck for you. All kinds of meat, fish, clothes, gadgets. And the air reeked of stinky tofu. And when it rained everyone would put up umbrellas, only there were so many of them people would poke each other in the eyes."

"What a scene."

"Yes," the woman chuckled. "My father remembered it so well. He would talk about it all the time, and other things from his childhood."

Chiang tried to imagine Shida night market years ago, long before Peak Heat.

"So ... you'll take money for it?" the woman asked.

"No, I'm sorry." Chiang put the photograph on the counter.

The woman frowned. She turned the photograph towards her.

"Perhaps you have something else?" Chiang

asked. "Look, I'll take half the price in money." he said. "That's fifty thousand dollars. If you pay the rest in something more reliable. I'm being generous."

The woman pressed her lips together. She felt in her pockets and pulled out a twist of thin paper. Opening it, she tipped two small gold earrings out onto her palm.

"Ah, that's better. Can I see them?" Mr. Chiang picked up the earrings, held up a magnifying glass and inspected them closely. "Nine carat. Not bad. I'll take them both. No need for any cash."

The man was leaning against a shelf in the corner of the shop, watching the transaction.

"No, no. Just one. I only want to spend one," the woman said.

"What? And split the pair? What good's one earring?"

"Maybe next week I'll come back and buy something else with the other one. You have so many wonderful photographs and antiques."

"Oh, you're too clever. All right, all right. One earring. And fifty thousand dollars."

"I thought you said forty thousand?" The woman smiled hopefully

"Ha!" Chiang waggled a finger at her. "Okay, forty-five thousand. Money's little use to me anyway."

Chiang dropped the earring into his safety box and put the woman's money in his pocket.

From the corner of his eye he saw the man approaching as the woman left. His face was grimy, and his hair was thick with grease. The shop now contained only the two of them. Placing his hands on the counter, the man leaned towards Chiang, who backed away from the reek of body odour.

"I hear you've got an old woman lives with you," the man said in a low voice.

Chiang's eyes met the man's level gaze. "Huh, of course not."

The man leaned closer.

"It's okay, I won't tell anyone."

Chiang shook his head, and stepped farther back. "The old folks who survived Peak Heat are all registered with the Government, you know that." Chiang pointed to the messages book the man had been examining. "If you're looking for a lost relative, you can look in there."

"There's thousands of notes in there. If I could just see her, this woman, I'd know if it's the one I'm looking for."

"Really, there's no old woman here."

"That's not what everyone's saying."

"I've told you the truth. Now, please leave. I'm closing the shop. I have to run an errand."

Shooting a hand over the counter he grabbed Chiang's arm. "It's my grandmother. You see, she wandered off one day, while I was asleep. Just a short time. I had to sleep, just for a short time ... and she was gone."

Chiang twisted his arm out of the man's

grasp and stooped to grab the baseball bat that was lying beneath the counter. When he rose, he held up the bat with two hands. The man stumbled back.

"I'm sorry, I didn't mean to ... I just wanted to -" He stepped towards the door, but as Chiang relaxed, he stopped.

"This is a strange shop," he sneered. "Where'd you get so many things?"

Chiang lifted the baseball bat a little higher. "I collect stuff."

"That's obvious." The man stroked a box of loose photographs with his fingertips.

"Leave that alone."

"Don't worry. It's not like I want to spoil your precious collection," he spat.

His fingers dropped to the base of the box, and Chiang ran from behind his counter. But before Chiang could reach the him, the man had flipped the box over and sprinted to the door. Chiang leaped over the scattered images and caught the door edge as it started to close behind the stranger. He sprang into the street, and immediately tripped and fell over the man, who was on the ground. In his haste to leave Chiang's shop, he'd apparently collided with a police officer.

Chiang's stomach turned at the sight of the officer. He leapt to his feet, and dragged up the man. The officer got up and straightened her clothes, and the two men bowed deeply again and again. Chiang was unable to take his eyes from the slim, silver stun stick that hung from her belt.

"What's the problem here?"

"No problem, officer, no problem at all," said Chiang.

"No, no problem," echoed the man.

Inside the shop, five minutes of questions pressed by the police officer elicited no more than a hastily generated story that the man was running because he was in a hurry, and that the photographs scattered on the floor were merely an accident. The officer sighed and looked from the man to Chiang and back again.

"Well, if you're in such a rush, you should go," she said. The man needed no further prompting. She turned to Chiang. "Are you selling that?" she said, her eyes on the baseball bat, which he was still holding.

Chiang chuckled weakly, sloped over to the shop counter and slipped the bat behind it. The officer spun on her heel, looking around the room.

"What an interesting shop. I don't think I've ever seen anything like it."

Chiang studied the floor.

"New businesses are springing up all over the place these days. It's wonderful. Every new shop I see, I think - yes, one more step on the road to recovery. Another stone in the wall of civilisation." She scanned a shelf spilling over with items.

Chiang glanced outside. The light was fading. Ching Yi would be home soon.

"So many different things. I don't know how to categorise them. What <u>kind</u> of shop would you say it is?"

"What? Oh, it's a – well, I've never really thought about it." Chiang rubbed his nose. "I just sell the things I've collected over the years. Just trying to make a living. Perhaps you'd like something? A freebie. As a thank you for ... for ... A donation, to the police force."

A corner of the officer's mouth lifted. She strode over to the messages book.

"What's this?" She leafed slowly through the pages.

"Just somewhere for people to write notes when they're looking for lost relatives."

"I see." The officer read aloud, "Chen Ke Le, looking for his father, Chen Kang Wei. Father, I'm living at Nan Jing East Road, Lane 24, Alley 11, Number 7. If you see this, please come and find us. We all miss you very much." The officer turned to Chiang. "I know what you sell."

"Yes?" Chiang heard his voice squeak.

"The past ... memories ... dreams. Of how things used to be."

Shaking his head, Chiang tried to think of something to say.

"You know, the Government has a great need for people like you."

Chiang studied the floor harder.

"How old are you?" The officer continued.

"Forty-five."

"Really? You look much older."

Chiang ran his fingers through his receding

hairline. "I've had a difficult life." He glanced quickly up. The officer's hair was streaked gray. She was probably about the same age as him. Who was she to be accusing him of being old, he thought. The woman's eyes became hard.

"Everyone's life is difficult these days. That's why the Government is making things better. Putting things back to how they were."

"Yes, yes." Chiang's shoulders drooped. He swallowed.

Putting down a juicer she had been examining, the officer placed her hands on her hips.

"You should come to the Government offices to help the staff with their work. Old gadgets are very useful for rediscovering forgotten technologies. And you, you must clearly know a lot of useful information."

"No, really, I'm just a collector. I don't know how half these things work."

"I've just told you you're in a good position to help in governmental efforts to improve society. Are you refusing to do your public duty?"

"Oh no, of course not. I wouldn't dream of —"

"Good. I'll return at ten tomorrow morning to collect you. I'm Officer Lin. Put together a selection of items you think will be most useful to the Government's cause. You'll be paid, of course. In money," the officer added, as if she were doing Chiang a great favour.

* * *

A terrible smell assaulted Chiang as he unlocked and opened the door to the living quarters behind the shop. The officer had stayed only long enough to accept the juicer that Chiang forced into her hands.

"Ma? Ma?"

An elderly woman sat slumped on a commode in a dimly lit, small living room. It contained little more than a broken down old sofa, two kitchen chairs and the commode. Photographs of old Taipei covered the walls.

"Ma." Chiang coughed and held his sleeve over his nose and mouth. "Ma, wake up." He raised his voice. "Wake up, Ma."

"Oh, oh, where am I?" the old woman mumbled as she stirred.

"You fell asleep again. Let me help you, Ma. Why didn't you ring your bell? It's right here."

"Oh, I don't like to bother you when you're working."

"That's silly, Ma. I don't mind. Here, let me clean you."

Forcing down the urge to retch, Chiang wiped the woman clean and helped her off the commode. He settled her in a chair and quickly closed the commode's lid.

"I'm so sorry, so sorry," the old woman murmured.

Chiang tidied the room. "Ma, I've told you

before many times. I don't mind helping you if you need me. Just ring the bell."

"It's not right. A man shouldn't help a woman. A daughter-in-law should help a mother-in-law. That's how things should be."

"Yes, well, there's no daughter-in-law here for you. So you have to make do with me, or Ching Yi. She'll be back soon."

"I used to have a daughter-in-law."

Chiang rummaged in a cupboard. The woman continued to talk in an inaudible mumble.

The door swung open and a pre-adolescent girl burst in. "What's that disgusting smell?"

Chiang placed a finger on his lips and motioned with his eyes to Ma. "You're late, Ching Yi," he said.

Ching Yi mouthed, "Oops, sorry." She swung her bag onto a chair. "I had to go the long way home. Someone had set up a stall selling fresh meat, and there was a big crowd. I was worried there would be a fight."

"You did the right thing. Now, it's nearly time for the night soil man."

Ching Yi grimaced. "Okay, okay." She pulled a cloth from her bag and tied it round her face. Head turned to the side, she removed the bucket from the commode and covered it with a lid. She retrieved another bucket from the bathroom, took them both outside. Twenty minutes later, she returned.

"Ah-ma, shall I comb your hair while Ba

makes dinner?"

"It's my daughter-in-law's job to care for me. I used to have one. Where is she? Where did she go? She shouldn't leave me here. I miss her. She was so good to me."

Ching Yi unwound Ma's bun and spread her gray hair over the back of her chair.

"It's so hot. Open the shutters," Ma said. "Open the shutters. I can't breathe."

Ching Yi looked at Chiang.

"Just a little. Let a little air in," he said.

She pushed one shutter door open and a brilliant, red-gold beam of evening light shone through the gap.

"It must be nearly six o'clock, Ba. Let's see if the electricity's on yet." Ching Yi sprang up and pressed the light switch. A single bulb blinked into life above their heads.

"Oh, quick, Ba, cook dinner while it lasts."

Chiang busied himself over a two-ring electric hob while Ching Yi slowly pulled a comb through the old woman's hair.

"Oh, that breeze feels wonderful. It's so hot in here."

"Is that nice, Ah-ma? Do you like the wind?" Ching Yi poured a little water out of a container onto a cloth, and wiped the old woman's face and neck.

"That's good. That's good."

"Ah-ma, we were talking about Peak Heat at school today."

The woman reached up, feeling Ching Yi's hands. Chiang turned to listen.

"Yes?" said the old woman.

"Well, I was wondering. It must have been terrible. How did you survive?"

"Ching Yi," Chiang snapped. "Have you been telling people about Ah-ma?"

"No, I haven't told anyone."

"Ching Yi." Chiang walked over and held up the girl's chin to look in her eyes. "You understand you must never tell anyone about Ah-ma. You understand?"

Ching Yi pushed the hand away. "I understand. I'm not stupid. I'm not a little, stupid girl."

"It was my son who saved us," the old woman said. "He was so clever. He should have been a doctor. Or a lawyer."

Chiang returned to the stove. "Why do you keep asking her the same question? You must have heard this story a hundred times."

"I like it. There's no harm."

"He built a small home for us, in an underground car park. Basement three I think it was. He sealed off part of it, so no one knew we were there. Just me, him, and my daughter-in-law. They had a baby coming. My grandchild." The woman clasped her hands together. "My first grandchild." Tears began to trickle from her eyes.

"You're upsetting her," said Chiang.

"Ah-ma, I'm your grandchild now, though,

aren't I?"

"Ching Yi," Chiang warned.

"Come here," said the woman.

The girl kneeled in front of Ma and guided the old woman's hands to her face. Her sightless eyes roaming, Ma's hands traced the lines of the girl's eyes and mouth while Ching Yi gently held her wrists.

"I'm your grandchild now."

"Yes, Ching Yi."

The girl lay her head on Ma's lap and the old woman stroked her hair. "We stayed in that little home a long time. It was so hot, even down there. And when my son or daughter-in-law came back from being outside, their skin was hot to touch. Aaaah ... " Ma sighed. "The baby couldn't survive, of course. But we lived. Us three in our little home. I went outside once, at night. The air felt like an oven. I didn't know how they could stand it, my son and daughter-in-law, going out to find food and water. They were very strong and brave."

"Like Ba," exclaimed Ching Yi.

"Yes, yes. But then food and clean water got more and more difficult to find, and they were gone for longer and longer—"

"Dinner's ready," said Chiang.

* * *

Chiang stared at the car Officer Lin drove over. A two-seater, it was boxy, high-roofed, silver and black and *new*.

Getting out and standing beside Chiang, the officer admired the car with him.

"Impressive, isn't it?" she said.

"I had no idea ..."

"That we had started manufacturing cars again? I know. Remarkable. And we've started to repair the roads. But wait until you get to the Government's headquarters. You'll be astounded at the progress they've made. You'll see why we must take every opportunity to help them in their work, regardless of personal sacrifice."

Chiang grimaced, and climbed into the vehicle. Officer Lin started the engine and told him to fasten a belt that went across his shoulder and hips. He wished he'd brought dark glasses and a hat to wear for the trip. Skirting potholes, weeds and piles of refuse, the vehicle brought stares from everyone they passed, and he knew his face would be remembered by all who saw it. He would become known as a police collaborator, if not a Government stooge. People would be reluctant to visit his shop.

Seeing the crumbling roadways and buildings brought back vivid memories of Chiang's childhood and youth, sleeping on hot, broken concrete floors, woken up by rats and cockroaches crawling over him, his parents dying of starvation and illness, nearly starving to death himself, and hiding, always hiding, from the people who looked at his skinny body with hungry eyes.

The tall spike of 101 drew closer as they travelled through the baking streets. Lin explained to Chiang how to open the car window to let in a cooling breeze, which blew away the nauseating smell of new plastic. Even so, he was sweating heavily by the time he entered the Government offices in 101. A chill blast of air brought his steps to a halt.

His eyes wide, he turned to Lin. "That's - ?"

"Air conditioning, yes," she said with a self-satisfied grin.

Feeling like a child, Chiang followed Lin through the entrance hall and into a lift. He touched the clean, shiny, metal walls and watched the floors count down on the display as they sank.

"What have you brought to be examined?" asked Lin, pointing at the bag Chiang was carrying.

"Oh, just a few bits and bobs. Some interesting objects. I don't really know anything about them, or how they work. "

Lin's eyebrow rose. "We'll see what the Government agents say. Perhaps they can help you add some more detail to your understanding of the artifacts you sell."

The agent who examined the pile of artifacts Chiang had brought was a young man with a large mole sprouting a tuft of long hairs on his cheek. He turned a mobile phone over in his hands. Chiang sat before him across a desk.

"Your name is Chiang Yin Xiong?" Chiang nodded. "Does this work?" The young man asked, holding up the phone.

Chiang rubbed his nose. "I don't know."

The agent pulled a power lead from the pile of objects on the table. He fitted one end into the phone and the other to a power socket on the wall. The phone lit up.

"If you didn't know whether it worked, why did you bring that lead along?"

Chiang silently cursed himself, forcing all expression from his face. "Both objects were together in a box. I thought perhaps there was some connection. I'm just trying to help."

The agent tssked. "You're saying you didn't try to connect the phone to a power socket?"

"Well, the supply is very erratic in our area—"

The young man stood up and hit the desk with his open hand. "The Government is doing everything it can to improve the electricity supply in all areas. Engineers are working day and night—"

"I'm sorry, I'm sorry, I didn't mean to imply—"

The young man sat down abruptly, and poked through the other objects.

Chiang had tried to put together a selection that included high technology items he couldn't possibly be expected to understand, such as the phone, and useless objects, such as a corkscrew and a picture holder. The agent pulled out a flat device with a screen that Chiang knew contained hundreds of works of fiction, and placed it on one side of the desk next to the phone. From beneath the pile he drew the largest object. Shaped like a wide, flat bat for hitting balls, the object's central area was a rusty wire mesh, and the handle held two buttons.

"I don't think I've seen one of these before. What does it do?"

Chiang shrugged. It was the one item that had actually completely confused him as to its purpose. He'd hoped the Government agents could tell him what it was.

"It's clearly electrical, but there's nowhere to attach a lead. Aha," said the young man as he popped open a cover, revealing an empty inner chamber. "This must house batteries. And there's a light bulb at this end. Some kind of flashlight? But it's too elaborate."

Chiang wiped his face, which was dripping despite the air conditioning. The agent frowned.

"You do know what this does, don't you? Why won't you tell me? What are you hiding?"

"No, no, really. I have no idea. Please. I want to help. I do. But I just collected these things." Chiang's throat tightened. "I'm just a collector."

Sneering, the young man threw the useless items into the bag Chiang had brought. "You clearly know more about these objects than you're telling us. But you'll remember." He turned to Lin, who was standing in the corner of the room. "I want an inventory of everything in this man's shop. Today." He stood up. "You won't sell any further items until we have given permission—"

"But, sir, it's my livelihood. How am I to live? I have a family to support."

"Don't worry. From now on, you're a Government employee, and you'll receive wages in cash every month. That's more than fair. You'll tell us all you know, and contribute to the effort of restoring a civilised society." The man smiled. "You should be proud."

Chiang lowered his head, and nodded. Lin took his unresisting arm and led him to the door then out into the corridor.

Chiang clenched his fists as they walked. Everything in his shop now belonged to the Government. And he was going to have to try to feed himself, Ma and Ching Yi on a cash income. He would find that man who had tipped over the box of photographs. This was all his fault.

"There's no need to look so glum," said Lin as they walked down the corridor. "He was right. You should be proud. Rebuilding our former society should be everyone's number one goal. We must return to how we were. Otherwise we'll continue living like animals, trying to survive from one day to the next."

Chiang listened with one ear. He was mulling over how to hide some his stock without Lin noticing when they returned to the shop. As she stopped dead, he looked up.

An old man had appeared around a corner of the corridor, leaning heavily against the wall with one hand and taking slow, staggering steps. Pyjamas clung to his bony frame, and he seemed oblivious to Lin and Chiang. Lin hesitated as the old man drew nearer. Chiang stared. He hadn't seen any old person but Ma for a decade or longer. A soft, tuneless hum buzzed from the old man's lips.

"Ah-gong, where are you going?" Lin asked, high and sweet.

The man stopped, as if noticing them for the first time. He gave no answer, but slowly backed up, bare feet sliding along the tiled floor.

"Let me help you, Ah-gong. You're lost."

The hum changed to a mumble Chiang couldn't make out. Increasing in volume as Lin drew nearer, her hand on the old man's arm turned the mumble into a shout. "I don't want to go back. Don't make me go back. I want to go and see my family."

"Now, now Ah-gong. Don't get excited. This is your home now. Come with me." Lin turned to Chiang. "What are you looking at, Mr. Chiang? Come here and help me with him."

Chiang walked slowly over to Lin, wondering at the abashed expression on the officer's face, and helped turn the frail man around. His protests grew fainter, until, weeping, he muttered, "I just want to go home." Lin guided the old man along the corridor, and knocked at a door. A plump nurse opened it. "Are you missing someone?" said Lin.

Chiang caught his breath. Through the

doorway the sweet, stale smell of old age drifted, and he saw grey-haired, wrinkled figures in sleepwear shuffling along or sitting vacantly in a large, windowless room.

The nurse took the old man's arms, drawing him inside. "Mr. Wu, where have you been? You're very naughty to run away like that. You'll get me into trouble." She glanced at Lin.

"This is a serious breach in security, nurse," said Lin.

The nurse bowed. "It won't happen again, officer, I assure you."

The old man pulled free of the nurse and tried to push past Chiang, who only half-heartedly prevented him.

"Mr. Wu. This is unacceptable," said the nurse as she grabbed the man's arms and pulled him in again.

"No, no, I don't want to go back. I don't want to go to the sleep room. I have bad dreams. It hurts my head," said the man.

"Oh Mr. Wu. Such nonsense," said the nurse. "It really doesn't hurt them at all," she said to Chiang. Lin pushed the man into the room and shut the door. The pair continued to walk, silence hanging between them. Lin's face was set and her eyes focused ahead.

"I know what you're thinking, but you're wrong," she said.

Chiang turned a stony face to her. "What am I thinking?"

Lin blushed. "You see ... you have to understand that the older generation are the key to the future. Only they can remember the time before Peak Heat. Only they have the knowledge we need to recreate the technological achievement of the past. So much was destroyed, lost or forgotten."

"The rumours are true, then? The Government has been taking old people and keeping them locked up?" Chiang couldn't keep an accusing tone out of his voice.

"Chiang, most of those people have no home and no family. Here, they're well looked after, kept cool and fed good food. And in return they help us rebuild."

Chiang snorted.

"What's so funny?" asked Lin.

"That old man was senile, demented. What could he or any of those other old folks possibly tell you that would be of any use?"

Lin cleared her throat. "Their minds still contain lots of information. It's just a matter of accessing it." Chiang stopped, and stared at the officer. Lin avoided his gaze. "Oh, it's just a simple thing. The nurse was right. It really doesn't hurt them."

"What doesn't hurt them?" Chiang tried to remain calm, but he spoke through his teeth.

"It's just deep brain reading. One of the few technological advances the Government managed to preserve intact throughout the Peak Heat collapse."

"Of course," said Chiang, bitterly.

"What does that mean?"

They stepped through the main doors into the street outside 101. Lin led Chiang out onto the empty, scorching road and placed a hand on his shoulder, turning him round.

"Look," she said, gesturing to the top of the mammoth building. It was a deep, dirty grey, and the lower windows were shattered. "Do you know what the plan is? Solar panels. Do you know what they are? They convert the sun's energy to electricity. From ground level to the tip, on all four sides. Enough electricity for the entire city, and more." She paused. "I know what the Government is doing with the older generation might seem disturbing or upsetting, but," she turned shining eyes to Chiang, "this is the kind of thing we must concentrate on now. The future."

Chiang ruminated on the way back to his shop. Civilising society was all well and good, but was it worth the cost? And did they really want a future based on a copy of the past? The past was pleasant to reminisce about, but it had also generated Peak Heat, which had led them to where they were now.

* * *

Chiang managed to hide the laptop that he'd been tinkering with behind his shop's counter, but it was impossible to prevent Lin from seeing and listing everything else in his shop. Going along each shelf, she painstakingly called out each item or asked him what it was if she didn't know. Every few minutes she checked that he was writing everything down. Worse still, Chiang had also been hearing the regular tinkle of a bell from the living quarters behind the shop.

Lin paused.

"I thought I heard a bell or something."

"Really? I didn't."

"Maybe it's someone selling something out in the street." Lin squatted to look at a shelf near the floor. The bell rang. She stood up. "There it is again. Are you sure you can't hear it?"

"Yes, I heard it that time," said Chiang. "You're right. It's from outside. Someone selling something, like you said."

Lin shrugged, and started to examine items on the low shelf. Chiang's heart rate slowed as the bell ringing stopped. Ma had probably fallen asleep again. But then it started, softly at first so that only Chiang could hear it, but gradually the sound grew louder and louder.

"Yin Xiong. I need a little help. Yin Xiong? Could you help me please? Yin Xiong."

Lin stood slowly up. Her wide eyes met Chiang's. "Who's that?"

Chiang sought for an answer.

"Yin Xiong. Are you there?"

"Chiang, who is that?" Lin turned to the door at the back of the shop. Chiang barely beat her to it. He spread himself across the door, facing the police officer.

"Please. She's just an old lady. She doesn't know anything."

"Step aside."

"Don't take her away. She can't help you. Let her spend her last years in peace."

"Move. Now." Lin drew her stun stick from its holster.

"Please."

The shop's front door creaked open. Chiang and Lin watched Ching Yi enter. The girl lifted her bag over her head, not noticing the scene. Then, "Oh." Her bag fell to the floor.

"Ching Yi, leave," said Chiang.

"Who's this?" asked Lin.

"My daughter. Please," Chiang's breath caught in his throat. "Please, she has nothing to do with this."

Lin replaced her stun stick in its holster.

"Thank you," said Chiang. Ching Yi backed towards the door.

"Stay there," said Lin.

"Yin Xiong?" Ma's voice came softly through the door. "Are you coming? If you're busy with a customer, I can wait."

"Let me through," said Lin.

"She's just an old lady," Chiang said.

"It's not ..." Lin pursed her lips, and seemed to search for words. "It's just ... this woman – is she your mother?"

"Yes. Well ..." He and Ching Yi looked at

each other. "No."

Lin put her hands on her hips and tilted her head. "No?"

Chiang sighed. "I ... I found her. She was alone. Starving. She had no one."

"Yin Xiong? I got into a bit of trouble. I can't stand up."

"Let me through!" Lin pushed Chiang to the side and wrenched open the door. She stopped on the threshold. Ma was sitting on the commode, staring blindly towards them. Lin leaned into the room, staring at the old lady. She turned to Chiang, her eyes full of tears.

"Yin Xiong?" Ma staggered up, trying to pull up her drawers with one hand while clutching the side of the commode with the other. Lin was by her side in a moment.

"Ma," she whispered.

The old woman's bottom hit the seat with a thump. "Who's that?"

"Let me help you," said Lin. She assisted Ma, and guided her across the room to the sofa.

"Who are you? Who are you?" The old woman felt upwards along Lin's arms as she lowered her into a chair. "I know you. I recognise your voice."

Lin's face crumpled as the woman's hands reached it. The thin, wrinkled fingers swept through tears.

"D – daughter-in-law? Is that you?"

Lin nodded.

"You've come back. You've come back at last."

"I've come back." She fell to her knees. "I'm sorry I took so long. Please forgive me."

"My son? Yuan Mao?"

Lin shook her head. "No, I'm sorry."

Chiang and Ching Yi hung back in the doorway, watching. Chiang motioned Ching Yi to step inside, and he pulled the door closed behind him. He waited while Lin and Ma hugged each other. After some time, Lin became aware he was watching her. She gestured to Ching Yi.

"This girl. Is she really your daughter?"

Chiang looked at Ching Yi, and shook his head.

"Mr. Chiang, you can't collect *people*."

"And *you* can't imprison them."

Lin stood up and smoothed her uniform. She placed a gentle hand on the old woman's shoulder. Chiang and Lin looked at each other, struggling to speak.

Ching Yi walked across to the old woman and took her hand. "Ah-ma, is this the daughter-in-law who used to look after you?"

"Yes, and she's come back. She said she would, and she did at last. She always kept her promises. I knew she would come back one day."

"But, Ah-ma, we're still your family too, aren't we? Ba and me?"

"Yes, yes, we're all family. You, Ba, daughter-in-law, and me. We're all family."

About the Author

British science writer and science fiction author J.J. Green writes about the frontiers of scientific exploration and wild fantasies beyond. Her fiction work has been published in Perihelion, the Mad Scientist Journal, Dark Tide Writers' Magazine, Metro Moms and other publications. Living in Taiwan has also given her endless opportunities to amuse the locals by attempting to learn Chinese. Check out her meanderings at infinitebook.wordpress.com

In the Mood

by
CK Hugo Chung

High noon in August was akin to a medieval dragon. Cantankerous and moody, the monster blasted out rays of heat that scorched the ground and drowned everyone in their own sweat.

Especially when you were dressed in a full combat uniform with a set of helmet, bayonet, daggers and mock grenades. Especially during break time when the whole garrison fell into soporific quietude and you, standing in the middle of the barrack square, had no surrounding traffic for distraction.

When closing your eyes, all you could hear were the dragon's droning roars, and your skin felt the burn from the cascading firefalls. They engulfed you and squeezed out every bit of sodium your body was able to hold

Where was your mind?

Heels tapping in the hallway reverberated
Sashayed forward as tremulous fabric undulated
The tender, alone and quiet, sent away
the hankering for unrequited attention, to one's liking
A shady corner guarded a secret, hot as Hades
wrapped in nocturnal sheath

I thrashed on the bunk bed restlessly. I stared at the twirling ceiling fan hoping its robotic movement could hypnotize me into nirvana.

I jumped up, paced back and forth, and sat down at my desk to read a bit of mawkish novella to calm down. Jitters, nevertheless, were stronger than ever. I knew you were out there, enduring. I wanted to step out, rush to you, hand you a piece of cold wet cloth, wipe off the dripping sweat from your delicate face, and assure you that everything would be all right. I wanted to plead — "let's screw this insane and ridiculous system, elope to find a place and live a life as a normal couple!"

But we were strangers then, one standing outside in punitive heat, another sitting inside grilled by a burning desire. Was I delusional to conjure up our chemistry?

I switched off the voice in my head, closed the book, laid down again, and pondered on why these lascivious fantasies inundated my mind. Was it libido? Was the dragon messing with me? I didn't want to have an iota of feeling for anyone. I just wanted to lay low, finish the obligatory term and move on. I didn't intend to cross *that* line.

I closed my eyes and tears welled up. I turned on my side and stared at some scraggy crack on the drab wall. I couldn't fathom how such conflicts tormented a poor boy with a pitiful secret.

Before I entered the two-year compulsory military service for every healthy Taiwanese male citizen, most of my friends had worried that my obdurate yet flamboyant character would hinder my safety in an environment that generally praised evangelic machismo. They had built their cases to argue that my delicate sensitivity was not cut out for the backbreaking training in the name of masculinity. They had even advocated that I should leave the country, to shirk the obligation, until its expiring age of thirty-five, or forever.

"Is that what you want? Bullied at best, or at the worst, beaten to death?"

I grimaced at their well-intended nagging, but developed the prescience that my instinct should help me weather through the unpredictable. Moreover, I had not come out to my family and desperately needed a change to get away from the post college reality. I wanted to use this time to clear my head, even if the military setup might not be equipped with any intellectual pursuits I was so used to feeling righteously entitled to.

Everything seemed to work out just fine, for a while.

After the orientation I was assigned to a logistics unit in northern Taiwan, a modest town named Qidu that traditionally served for the country's second largest seaport, Keelung, where a prominent navy force was based. The place then was dull as dishwater with sleepy streets and pathetic looking shops.

Being part of a boutique operation of less than 100 staff members, I didn't get to experience any exciting practices such as crawling through mud, nor did I perform any intense physical duties. As a Private at the lowest rank I started my days by scrubbing down the bathroom urinals and serving meals for the higher echelons. Our seemingly insignificant unit was filled with the repetitive routines: Morning Reveille at 5:30 A.M., breakfast at seven, inventory check-in around ten, lunch break at noon, various training drills in the afternoon, dinner at 6 P.M., evening propaganda classes until nine, followed by Night Formation and a curfew. On weekends there was the so-called Maintenance during which the unit staff was kept bare bone and we got some free time without leaving the unit.

I couldn't care less for these boring duties. My plan was to stay alert for personal safety, at the price of dumbing down any singular intelligence. Blending in would enable my subsisting through this peculiar period. I butlered my way up by following orders with discretion and keeping my head down as a hypocrite. I dodged the rampant bullying scenes among my peers. I acted like a sponge to soak up other comrades' mental dramas without giving away my true identity. They jokingly nicknamed me "Tsai Buei," a Taiwanese term for a pushover guy who never minds picking up others' leftovers or dirty laundry.

Despite some rare occasions of being hazed in those first few rookie months, through credibility and shrewdness, a year later I rose to the rank of Corporal to manage a tiny team of seven Privates. As I gained my footing, I also realized that the military, like everywhere in the world, was a Machiavellian game: I was compelled to establish a certain status to maneuver and manipulate others, higher or lower than my rank regardless, for survival. I played it well, cunningly, opportunistically.

Until I met you. You were not a game.

I. Smoke Gets In Our Eyes

Mood never ceased to solicit
Vibrancy seeded in fluttering hearts
Millennium seemed a miraculous volcano
Sedation of the indolent awakened and came alive
Eyes, skins, alchemy of emotional audacity

prompted a subtle passing of firefly's sparkles in a
dark forest

He was a Corporal as well. Starting as a
Private six months prior to my arrival, when our
unit was going through the transition from Air
Force to Army.

The Air Force had a notorious reputation for
tougher hazing against newbies, especially among
those antichrist AFCs (Airman First Class). They
didn't give a hoot about any consequences. They
ran wild and looted everyone's minimum respect in
the name of fostering masculinity.

He suffered a great deal of the harsh
treatments from those seniors of the former regime:
the constant verbal abuse and intermittent physical
violence had made him feel like a downtrodden
street rat, second-guessing his every move. Once he
was ordered to do one hundred push-ups, in
skimpy undergarments in a freezing winter night, at
one of the so-called "midnight drills" when a group
of drunk AFCs randomly plucked and dragged out
a rookie from his sleep, and tortured him on the
rooftop of our dormitory building. He even got a
kick in his stomach because he snorted at a wasted
senior who had called him a faggot.

Neither a college graduate nor dandy
intellectual, he didn't have the capacity required for
being a military service manager. Getting yelled at
all the time in our unit, he somehow hung on by a

thread through his pledged loyalty to a small clique of fellow Corporals. They were the rat pack of five members bonding over the beginner's torture, and making up for it later by acting out like obnoxious gangsters busting everyone's balls.

He was the quiet one compared with those boisterous clowns. He liked to ruminate on serious topics about life. He liked to talk precociously as an old man even though he was younger than most of his peers. He liked English, considered fancy in the unit, and tried to practice it by himself whenever he could. I once bumped into him reciting an English dictionary while serving the night duty of surveillance.

He drank like an old school sailor to cultivate his articulation. But in an inebriated miasma he always blurted out some gibberish that got everyone flummoxed as if a drunk uncle slurred improper secrets at a family gathering.

We passed by each other in the office, stood next to another in a cafeteria line, and crawled side by side under the barbed wires during a routine drill. I couldn't take my eyes off him every time when our paths crossed.

His eyes were inscrutably dark and melancholy, contrasting prominently against his alabaster skin. His gangly figure looked fragile at times, but showed no sign of being weak. He was the delicate and pretty boy he never intended to be.

He was the Tazdzio in my *Death in Venice*.

His beauty, untapped yet precious, cast a spell to dazzle me, weakening my knees to fall and worship.

The more I observed from afar, almost like a stalker, the more profoundly his aura haunted and stirred up some indescribable essence within myself. I wasn't sure what that was. Every attempt to define and rationalize my feelings toward him made little sense. They were instinctive and primordial beyond reasoning. They were the knocks on the door, the rush out of involuntary feelings, and the release from a cage.

Our first encounter was less than ideal.
He singled me out to meet him in an alley after lunch break. First I was excited as we had never spoken before. I arrived there only to find out he wanted to flex his muscles. Someone from the rat pack had thought that I, as a junior colleague, seemed to have an easy time with the authority, enjoy the privileges as a team leader, and had not been tamed enough to show other comrades the respect they deserve.

After a makeshift speech about ethics and manners, delivered nervously and poorly due to lack of alcohol, he ordered me to get down for some pushups at his will. I wasn't going to refuse, but his attitude, like a funky sibling fussing over trivialities, triggered my latent rebellion.

I looked up to shoot him a beam of disappointment.

"What are you staring at?"

His retort was accentuated by those amazingly deep eyes. The air was thick with silent tension.

I gotta do what I have to do to appease my people.
I understand. I just hoped you would be different.

That was our first unspoken exchange, only by the hearts. We knew it would become our shared tongue.

Afterwards he never called me out again in public. However, every time our gazes met, anywhere in the unit, I could feel the subtle invitation.

Something changed. Some feelings, for each other, were gentler and murkier.

I secretly welcomed the shift but had no clue how to make an advance. He never overtly promised anything, but his eyes never stopped implying. I tried very hard to figure out his obscure coding.

How would I begin? Would he step back if I just moved forward? Did I overanalyze his message, as I always did when facing the allure of a stranger?

I'd had physical contacts with men. I'd had platonic romance with men. I never had the combination. I was never open with myself about the need to be loved. At times my body was arbitrarily at others' disposal. Self guardedness was a wall I built internally despite a façade of easy access via external touch.

But he, the first one, had me swing a shovel to break the ground and build a bridge for two wretched souls reaching out, in mysterious ways, to connect.

That summer dragon was our witness. Its heat simmered to levitate the veil. The azure sky, cloudless, was the limit.

What's restrained got harder to be contained
Let it fly, let it be sneered at
heartbeat could not lie / mistake had its own device
Tried to stay alive

I stood at the other side of the door, trying to steady my breathing after a short sprint. With a mosquito screen in between, our eyes met.

What are you doing over there? Come in.

Like a wearily defeated king, he feebly held out his fingers to motion. I pushed the door open, excitedly, gingerly, nervously. No one was around. He reclined on the bunk bed like a balloon out of air.

"What did you do to piss off the Chief Commander?" I spoke softly while stepping toward his bed. I lit a cigarette and watched the oozing smoke pirouette in the irresistible sunlight, which was pouring a tempered golden flood into the room.

"He was in a bad mood, bossed around and picked on anyone to his dislike during Maintenance.

I happened to be there as a scapegoat."

His raspy voice sounded vulnerable. His face, drained yet chillingly cold, stopped me from any pointless prying.

"Are you all right?"

I knelt down and leaned my head next to his feet.

He grimaced at my silly question.

A Sunday afternoon, off duty and bare bone, brimmed with laidback ease like a jazz concert in a park.

Time, eternal yet fleeting, stopped momentarily for the quietude.

I could hear my inner voice shooting millions of questions back and forth as I eagerly wanted to learn who he was, figure out what we were, and come up with some idea of where we could go from here.

He gently stroked my hair and sighed, again and again. I felt warm as a tear trickled down on my face.

I took it, all of it, with a grain of salt.

"Why do you think we are here?" He lit a cigarette and stared at the floor, drowned in a dusky river.

"So we get to meet properly?" I was reckless. He cackled.

I grabbed his cig and took a deep drag. Our fingertips touched. The smoke flowed out of my nostrils, extremely flimsy, to underscore our sprouting affinity.

I looked up to meet his eyes. He looked right back for a second but instantly flicked away. His cheekbones stood out prominently in a five o'clock shadow, driving me to lose my mind.

"What are you going to do after your service is over?"

Not ready to give up, I felt like I could handle him playing hard to get.

"I don't know. Perhaps find some place that fits me the best."

"And where will that be?"

"I don't know. A small town where I can be anonymous." He took a deep drag of cigarette.

He wanted to fly away like I did. He wanted to settle down quietly like I did. We were very much on the same page about the future. I didn't need to say anything anymore. I was too enamored, too horny.

For the rest of afternoon we smoked more cigarettes and listened to a CD filled with the oldies such as *Those Were the Days*.

No need to push for any more clearance for now, it wouldn't make sense anyway as neither of us had any idea how this epiphany would carry on. All we could recognize was we kept each other company in that room of magical intimacy.

Do you think we can do this?

Who knows? Do you want to give it a shot?
Why not?

The evening crept up, the staff on weekend leave gradually returned to the unit, and Night Formation was about to start as the last order of business for the day to make sure a complete force was in place. We had to get dressed for it but we were somewhat reluctant. Out of the blue his rat pack stormed into the room, drunk and loud, broke our union. We jumped away from each other.

"Get the hell out of here, Stupid! That's enough for today!"

His closing was awkward and clunky. I played along and left in a fake slouch. On the way back my mind was swimming in full joy, already planning for the next move, not realizing that one member from the pack followed me out and squinted his eyes like a predator.

I knew I could be the promise he was too craven to keep out in daylight but clandestinely lusted after in a dream.

Hope was an aphrodisiac I was hopelessly addicted to.

The maudlin, corny as it was, laid out the serenade
for the hearts too shy to speak
Not plighted to lyrical rhymes
The poetry must come out
suited only for the beaten, sans the expository

to find a momentary shelter

II. Those Were Our Days

Summer night rolled out in front of us as if it were a magical carpet, riding high tides along the shore. Its embedded stars aligned to exude sparkles.

We could hear the soothing repeats from ocean waves below us and the underlining of their soft whisper —

Could we really have our way?

The Sergeant Major from our unit, in his mid 40s, a fishing fanatic and raging alcoholic, had sensed our burgeoning connection from one evening's off-duty drink binge. He never asked any questions. Instead he shrewdly set up a private outing to a sleepy village near the town Suao in Yilan County.

I had no idea how he stumbled across our relationship nor his true feelings about it. Despite being wildly popular among my peers in the unit (due to his inbred connectedness with the unit's authority and his personal generosity of treating everyone coming in his door with a shot of whatever alcohol was served), he kept us under the radar so that no one in the unit could be aware of this exclusive invitation.

We maneuvered diplomatically to get on the same vacationing schedule without raising anyone's suspicion. Both of us were grateful for the Sergeant's discretion. Fussy as such arrangement might get, it was a small price.

He picked me up at the crack of dawn. I was exhausted from lacking sleep in the previous night. We were silent on the drive to meet the Sergeant.

Aren't you happy to see me?

I am. Just too tired from last night's excitement. And anxiety.

Why?

You know why. Don't make me say it.

If you behave well today, I might have a gift for you.

I turned to look at him, feeling amused by his insinuation, and my lethargy bid adieu.

The second we arrived at the pier, surrounded by the slanted cliffs of Seashore Mountain Range, we were stunned by its unique character. It was such an off the beaten path kind of place where bona fide fishing mavens congregated. The magnificent Pacific Ocean presented its grandiosity in a lambent move. The breeze was salty and sultry. The sun slow-cooked the air with a comfortable amount of heat and minimum humidity. Rows of industrial breakwaters, made out of cement, were casually lumped together. They were usually intense and inappropriately ugly for seaside scenery, but today they looked relaxed and cordial in daylight.

We chose a spot that overlooked currents, carried on small talk throughout the day, and felt awkwardly restrained at times in front of the Sergeant, out of respect.

Both of them were keen at angling and wanted to try trawling on a motorboat. They competed for techniques, chugged down chilled beers, and let down their guards momentarily to take joy in old school male bonding.

Not an outdoors buff, I had zero knowledge and no real interest in their talk. I sat beside them and daydreamt often. While they patiently waited for the rods' tips to start moving, I read a book or jotted down some random thoughts on life. I was concerned about coming out, but couldn't help but wonder how our future might take off from this moment: What should we do for the next date? Would have been nice with just two of us. Even lovelier if he showed up with some flowers.

The day proceeded in ease. I enjoyed the comfort of being absentminded and carefree. My smile lingered in that lovely late summer day.

A fisherman made every attempt to lure the desired
commanded a village to reap the reward
declared that love came from the alchemy
of bygones, never the unknowns
Dropped memory, shed denial, celebrated the
revelation
of intimacy, eternity, transparency

Audacity was the blessing with no disguise

As the evening snuck up, the Sergeant wisely left us to attend his family dinner. Some diehard klatsch of fishing veterans still lolled around, but most were gone by then.

Even with just the two of us, he still wouldn't relax, acting more rigid than the concrete we sat on. He looked ahead into the recondite ocean, dark and unpredictable, brooding over the things I hardly understood and had no access to. I ventured to lay my head on his bony shoulder and wrap my arm around his. To my surprise he didn't push away. Breathing slowly in the dark, we were waiting for a catch, in this evanescent yet self-contained bubble which was our first date.

"Do you think we can get away with it?"

My tone was tender yet weary. I couldn't imagine the consequence if our affairs were to be found in the unit. He would have escaped it more easily than I did because of the rat pack's protection. Out there as I was, I might end up as a martyr, or a scapegoat, at the mercy of others' prejudice.

"I don't know. I don't want to think about it." He was unruffled.

"How can you not?" I was annoyed.

"I trust the Sergeant. I think we will be OK."

"Really? How can you be so sure? As far as I am concerned there's no guarantee."

"What kind of guarantee do you want?"

"I don't know. What are we even doing right now?"

His indifferent tone propelled my insecurity. I detached myself from him.

Suddenly he turned to my face and bestowed a sweet gift. It lasted about fifteen seconds. The salty sea air truly softened his lips.

The stars were our cheering crowd. The waves were our symphonic coda.

In ecstasy, in surprise, in every line the universe intended to inspire.

My eyes opened to meet his. Eternity presented itself in his profound gaze. He held my hands, rubbed them gently around his cheek for a second, and let go softly.

I would have liked to ask for another kiss, but I didn't.

The spellbound sweetness coming from his mysterious aura was too pithy for my understanding. I felt he finally allowed my presence in his mind.

We stayed there until the wee hours. He drove me to my home and spent the rest of night there.

Winter passed
Mood rose
Thoughts felt brighter
Actions moved faster
Those were our days when

I stepped on the pedestal to confront my messy life
You emerged from the icy thick white and smiled
We finally
say hi

We talked every night on the phone. He had to keep his voice low because of rooming with the rat pack. My arrangement was better as I was assigned to a single room.

I could accept what we had to live with, but I did not feel like staying on the same course with no definition.

Am I yours?
Aren't we talking?
I just need you to say it, one more time.

Like a superbly self-conscious and self-centered high school kid, I demanded a lot of verbal confirmations from him without being sympathetic to our context. He was always reluctant to say anything committal, driving me frantic. My hysteria was relentless at his withheld disinterest. He tried to point out the difficulty of being in our environment but I refused to hear any of it. In my mind I wanted him to hold his head high, to face the music that didn't play beautifully to our ears. What I didn't realize was I never followed my own advice to come out. I was still hypocritically cagey and dodgy around everyone in the unit, but I kept pushing him to open up so everyone could roll out the red carpet to welcome us.

It was wishful thinking, and delusional.

Our days in the military were usually filled with solitary moments between duties. When alone, I kept making mental reminders that I should not be with a weaker guy. But when he passed by, when our fingertips lightly brushed against each other's, the beauty that was everything he oozed, trapped me blind and fed my addiction like opium.

While I was tortured by my own brewing mental dramas, he took in everything reservedly. He chose to stick around because he saw something in me. He felt it was all right to share his true ambition with someone outside the rat pack, in whom he had full trust. He wanted to start his own business after leaving the service. He wanted to speak English well. He told me he could use a partner.

"But how do you see me in this? Will I be the one?" I said yes on a good night, but flipped on a bad one. He fell silent on the other side of the phone.

I reached out to a nearby bottle, Kingman Sorghum, a popular cheap moonshine found in any military unit.

Frustrated and wordless, both of us started drinking while staying on the phone. We heard the alcohol-drenched burps from each other.

Our struggle lasted for about four months, inside and outside the unit. I developed a daily mantra: "I am going to leave him today".

I failed, as always.

I was lovelorn as his nonchalance gave me nothing to stay hopeful. And yet he returned every night to ask for my affection. I gave him what he wanted and put aside my own needs. I thought that was how it would work. It was condescendingly foolish of me to surmise that I could be the savior in this relationship. I cooked up the theory that as long as I kept trying hard: where there was a will there should be a way.

One night I invited the majority of the rat pack to my room for some bonding time. My own interactions with them had fared better due to my increasing seniority around the unit. I also presumed that such change might arrive from his defense, although I never knew what he actually said about me in front of them.

He didn't show up in my room to avoid any tangential speculation. I was disappointed.

Toward the end of night, after countless sorghum shots, I became too drunk to care. I got loud with the pack, mimicking their obnoxious manners and vulgar banters. For a second I felt I blended in so well and my guard came down finally.

Past midnight, I called him up, for our routine check-in. Intoxicatingly wasted, I giggled flagrantly like a schoolgirl. The rest of them toned down the conversations so they could listen to us, not knowing their most trustworthy buddy was on the other end, to dig up some dirt from me.

At one point I got bored by our conversation and carelessly dropped my cell phone on the desk to use the restroom. One member from the pack frivolously picked up the phone and tried to play pranks. But when he spotted the number on the screen, he froze.

After coming back from the restroom, I realized my phone had been in his best buddy's trembling hand for a while. The guy was astonished and the rest of them were disarmingly quiet. Feeling mortified and quickly sobering up, I snatched the phone back only to find out it was disconnected. I threw everyone out, calling it a night.

It was too late. They already knew. They left in silence.

I called him back. He answered in great furor.

"How can you leave me like this???"

Equally drunk, his pitch was frenziedly high at first but abruptly dropped. I guessed the pack was back. He solemnly admonished that we needed to stay low for now.

"I am sorry I did this. I am sorry because I am so in love with you!"

I felt a bout of relief after hearing myself say it. My confession might be a loser's move, but there was never a rule when a heart wanted to speak out.

Loving was easy, love was not
All promise, expected bright and compact
for the everlasting
Holding on was efficient and genuine
patience took time
Couldn't make it work for now
What was the purpose if nothing mattered?
The prayer was never answered

III. In the Mood for Love

"Well, this is not going to work"

The Sergeant Major lit a cigarette, and stared at me.

He had summoned me to his private chamber after lunch break, when the whole unit fell into the silence of the scheduled siesta time.

"What do you mean?" I squeezed out a smile, trying to act casual. He sighed and blew out a thick stream of smoke.

"Listen, just stay low. You should know better that some people in our unit might find out what your relationship is and make a fuss about it."

"Someone said something?" I lit a cigarette, took a few more drags, and felt slightly stunned by his straightforward statement.

"Maybe." He sighed again.

"Will I be in trouble?"

"Not if you act like this."

"Why are you protecting us, especially me?"

Chin up, arms back, I snubbed out the cig

butt and stood straight to face him. He shook his head with a grimace.

"Listen, you are smart and savvy, although sometimes too much for my taste, but anyway, who am I to judge? What you are doing now, especially in this unit, is no good for anyone." His tone dropped, and I felt that his laser severity, out of genuine concern, tore me apart. I was fidgeting and trying to come up with some new defense for us.

"What do you think I should do?"

"Well, the first thing you can and should do is to stay distant until the rumor passes. He is not as strong. He is very confused. Give him some time and space. Will you?"

I left the Sergeant's room, shivered and felt more insecure than ever. What were the people saying behind our backs? How serious was the rumor? How could I face these people after the siesta?

Million of questions with few answered, I spent the rest of that day making up my mind not to see him. But such delusion would never succeed. The next morning during the reveille, we exchanged glances during a routine march. He pulled back, and I was frustrated.

"What is our future?" One late night, I brought up this question during our check-in, drunkenly desperate.

"I really don't know. I plan to move to China.

Can you come with me?"

"Why China? I am going to New York afterwards. I don't know. Why don't you come with me?"

"That's impossible. I have to think about my career."

"What about us?"

Both of us fell silent, not willing to make room for each other's plans, and it kicked off the ensuing period of our détente. A tug of war in hearts.

I was imprudent and impatient. I thought I was prepared to throw everything out of the window, open up our relationship to the unit and confront the consequences. The Sergeant failed to persuade me further and gave up on my stubbornness.

Now all I could do was to have the boy on board with it.

He said nothing, frozen as Antarctica.

Frustrated and sullen, I started to make demands for him to prove his commitment to our relationship, such as coming out to the rat pack. He snorted and called me crazy; I retorted by naming him a fool. We were often at odds, stirring up the tension to affect everyone around.

The rat pack, always frowning upon our connections, kept mum and gloated.

By the time he was ready to leave the service,

I still had six more months left, but our relationship had gone south for a while. He was always aloof during the day in front of the whole unit, which infuriated me, but we still talked every night, which made me believe we still genuinely cared for each other.

A week prior to his departure, one morning I stopped by his room. I had seen a profile picture of him in earlier days, handsome as Dorian Gray, and I wanted to ask for it as a souvenir.

He flat out refused with some lame excuse, such as that this was a dangerous move for leaving a trace, which was nonsense. We had a huge fight and I left there begrudgingly and swore never to see him again. A few days later he received the certificate of retirement from the military. I was very upset because we didn't depart on good terms. I called him later that day to make peace.

We didn't say much as he was out celebrating with the rat pack. They all left the military together. When I called, he happened to have a stripper sitting on his lap.

He stopped her advances and stepped out to accept my call.

I miss you. What happened to us?
You tell me.
This is torture. I really can't deal with your being noncommittal.
What do you want? We have different plans.
Will I see you again now that you are moving to

China?
Come see me outside the unit. We'll talk.

On my next vacation I took the train from Taipei for Taoyuan, his hometown, to meet him. We picked a quiet café for the conversation, eye to eye with speechless regret.

I am sorry. It is what it is.

He blushed, out of feeling embarrassed. I choked up, out of feeling selfish.

But then his business partner in China suddenly appeared. He was sent by one of the rat pack members to talk about "the plan" for the future.

Our conversation was reduced to desultory small talk, pushing me over the edge of a cliff. I decided to leave such pretension and rushed out, feeling dizzy.

On the commuter train back to Taipei my heart was inundated with unspoken sorrow. I thought that might be the last time.

My heartstring was torn apart into million threads.

I willfully refrained myself from making any more contact. I thought he had already moved away and I would try my best to start afresh for the next chapter.

On Valentine's Day, I was serving the duty of daytime vigilance. I got an unexpected phone call from a familiar voice —

"What's up?" At the other side he sounded quite lighthearted.

"Are you still in Taiwan?" I was trembling.

"My last day. Fly out tomorrow. I am calling to say goodbye."

During the curfew in the same evening, I called him up. My cell phone battery was low then.

Have you packed?

Not really, my flight will be late so I'm just fiddling and procrastinating.

I can't take this anymore. I am going to leave you for good.

People in my life just decide they can come and go, never bother to ask me how I feel.

You have to live with it. Maybe someday we will see each other.

I will never forget you.

We were silent, for a long time. The white noise of his background TV ebbed and flowed between our intermittent sighs.

I want to tell you a story, from the movie, "In the Mood for Love" —

In Cambodia, near Angkor Wat, there is a tree that accommodates everyone's sorrowful secrets. All you have to do is to find a cavity on the trunk, tell your secret in, and stuff it with mud and wild grass. Your agony is left there forever. You will leave there as a happy person.

I am not sure I will be happy.

Please remember me in your secret, no matter

what –

My phone died completely right at that second.

It was so dead that I had to give up and purchase a new model a few days later. When the new phone was charged and turned on, his number was erased, gone. I never heard from him again.

Wanting to have all was not sinful
Speaking out could be wronged as impudence
only if induced from the soulful
Struggling to strike the equilibrium bearing
A consequence of the mouthful, lurching to grab
everything
to live in the blissful
The melancholy of not getting lingered
The sentiment never departed fully
Go round and round, the mood seemed within
reach
Existed as a poignant line of phantasm

I tried to stay strong after the break-up. But my heart was so traumatized that it denied everything. Numb and cheerless, I could hardly put myself together. My family eventually discovered my secret, outed me, and caused a scene no less similar to a nighttime soap opera, full of unbearable yelling and heartbroken tears. Ultimately they would accept me as their son, but never a shameful homosexual. They suggested that I move away for a while so that everyone could get piece of mind.

I became an ostracized black sheep. My sorrow found no tree trunk to fill.

I had no damn to give. I returned to nameless corporal warmth to survive through the cold reality.

A few years later, one August, I happened to travel to Cambodia on vacation.

At high noon, cantankerous and moody, as the dragon still blasted out rays of heat no one could bear, I woke up in a tragically cramped hotel room, near Angkor Wat, with a nameless stranger snoring next to me.

I sat up and looked around, and suddenly it dawned on me that I once loved a boy.

He was the true love of my life. I once dreamt we would see each other here and shared the stories of our life, after all these years.

Now I was in no mood. The beauty was gone forever.

I had moved on from the story. But I was more lost than ever.

I hugged myself and began to cry.

About the Author

CK Hugo Chung is Taiwanese by nature and a lifelong New Yorker by nurture. Writing in both Chinese and English, his essays and short stories can be found in various bilingual publications. He is the co-founder of a writer's collective, Writeous, and an active member of Taipei Writers Group. Currently he is the Assistant Editor for GOAT magazine, and Contributor at Large for Vogue Taiwan.

Dragon's Call

by
L.L. Phelps

When Lara moved to Taipei, dragons were
the last thing on her mind, as was everything else in
the magical realm. It was true this was unusual, as
she was a seer, a caretaker of the magical creatures
most believed to be myth or fairy tale, but leaving
home to teach English in Asia had been meant as a
way of escape from all she knew. She had been
trained at the New England Seer Academy to deal
with all levels of magical problems, from wide
spread sighting crises to troll and alien creature
uprisings, yet the biggest problems she had faced
since taking over the seership of her family estate
were nothing more than trivial squabbles. Most
considered her lucky to have inherited such a job,

which was far less dangerous and demanding than the public caretaking jobs required of most seers, but Lara felt restless and increasingly annoyed at the problems her job required her to address. She accepted it as her fate, something she had always been reminded of growing up, but she wasn't sure she was ready to face such a life, and had decided to walk away from it. At least temporarily.

Lara knew when planning her move that Taipei would have inhabitants of its own in the magical realm. It was an island host not only to legendary Chinese creatures, but lesser-known fairies and a unique collection of beings tied to aboriginal Taiwanese culture, and a handful of creatures from Japan and other countries whose people had occupied the island at certain points in its history. Lara was curious about these creatures, but set on maintaining an indifference towards their presence. As long as she did not make an effort to look for them, they would remain concealed from her vision by spells used as a precautionary measure in large cities against renegade seers who walked outside the tight reign of the Universal Council and their unbending Laws. It seemed the perfect situation for Lara, and everything lined up for a few years of normalcy. At least as normal as it could get for a blonde haired, blue-eyed American joining the ranks of expat English teachers in Asia.

After two weeks of exploring, Lara knew it was time to get a job and a place to live. She found an apartment through an online ad, a German male and Canadian female seeking a roommate. The rent was reasonable and the location decent, so Lara made her move. When she arrived, the first thing she did was peer past any concealment spells for creatures the two potential roommates may have unknowingly brought with them from their native countries. Seeing none, she looked the place over, and after examining her room, paid Hans and Maggie a deposit. She moved her suitcase from the hotel later that day, and then went out to buy linens. When she returned to the apartment that night, it was dark and calm, the only sound in her room the steady traffic and occasional screech of the metro train, commonly known as the MRT, as it passed in front of the building.

Lara had seen when accepting the room that her window faced the aboveground portion of the MRT, but that had been one of the reasons she had decided on the apartment. At home there'd been train tracks not too far from her family's estate, so there was something comforting about that vague tie to the familiar. She'd only been away for a couple of weeks, but she was already starting to feel a bit homesick, especially for the cook, Betty, and gardener, Joe, who had practically raised her after her parent's disappearance years before. Both Betty and Joe had understood her need for space when she had announced she was leaving, but it was clear that at least Betty disapproved of her sudden departure.

"You can't escape who you are," Betty had

told her that last night on the family estate.

"I can't escape it, no," Lara had said. "But I can take a break from it, can't I?"

Betty had looked uneasy at first, then smiled knowingly. "I guess it's really not that unexpected. Your dad did this same thing once, running away."

"Gee," Lara had said, her tone sour. "A shame he's not here now to tell me how that went."

Betty had looked pained, as she always did when Lara expressed her bitterness towards her parents' absence. "Ask your grandmother, Lara," she had replied softly. "She can tell you plenty."

"She refuses to speak of him."

"I think she would if she knew you were leaving. Maybe you should take a trip to see her before going through with your plan."

"I'm not going to New York," Lara had said, tossing the last of her clothes on top of her suitcase and searching for a second bag for her books. "Anyway, if I told her I was leaving the country, she'd only try to guilt me into staying. She wants me to be a private seer here until I'm old and grey like her. A prisoner."

"You're an heir, is all," Betty had said in her cheerful way. "Like a princess."

Lara had given her a dark look. "Being a private seer is nothing like being a princess."

Now, weeks later in Taipei, Lara wondered if her grandmother knew yet that she had left. She was sure some of the creatures had already made their way to New York to report her, if Betty or Joe hadn't gotten through first by phone. Regardless, Lara was determined not to care. Her grandmother had email, she had Skype, so if she had something to say, she could figure out how to use one of the two like a normal adult and contact her. Not that it would do her any good. She'd have to let one of Uncle Frank or Great Aunt Marta's kids take up the post for a while. Lara only hoped the estate's creatures would be accepting of the change.

Lara was lost in these thoughts until well after midnight, and almost missed the strange sound that came from outside. But then it came again, a high whistling combined with a low, rumbling growl. It made her hair stand on end, a clear sign that it had something to do with the invisible realm, which was odd considering the concealment spells that should have shielded her from such things. She wanted to ignore it, but she knew her seer instincts would allow her no peace if she tried.

With a sigh of annoyance, Lara slipped out of bed and crossed the room to the window. It was calm outside, the traffic sparse in the early weekday hour. The MRT had shut down, but when the sound came again, it was on the MRT station two blocks away that Lara's eyes settled. She squinted, trying to get a good view of the darkened structure, but as soon as her eyes met the noise's source, her heart sank.

It was a dragon.

And not the type of dragon she'd often seen

passing through her family's estate. This was a Chinese dragon. Long like a serpent, red and black, it rose into the air, slithering from head to tail, and slipped into the clouds in the dark sky before making its way back down to the yellow pavilion roof of the station. There waiting for it was a figure clothed in black, its face covered like a ninja from a movie. When the dragon rose again, the figure threw its hands up, and the beast twisted mid-air and came back down.

"What in the..." Lara opened the window to get a better view. She wondered if she should go to the station and find out who the figure was, to learn the reason the dragon was making itself visible and audible to any seers in the city. Instinctively, she wanted to make sure the dragon was safe, not imprisoned by a renegade seer, but after watching for several minutes, it was clear the creature was not in any distress. Eventually it made a final plummet towards the MRT station, and then took off towards the mountains. As soon as it was out of view, Lara made her way back to her bed, her seer instincts satisfied. The dragon was safe, cared for by seers no doubt abiding by the Laws of the Universal Council, leaving her under no obligation to look into the matter further.

* * *

Lara had a job interview the next day at a school downtown. She dressed in her best, and grabbed her degree and papers, all the while composing an imaginary interview in her mind to distract herself from the magnetic memory of what she had seen the night before. As she reached the MRT station, however, her eyes began an involuntary search for the dragon, peering past the light veil of potential concealment charms. She nearly tripped as she made her way up the stairs to cross the bridge to her platform. She scanned the ceiling and walls of the station to see if the creature was using a chameleon effect to blend in, or perhaps a stone charm to look like a statute, as she had heard Asian beasts were prone to do. It wasn't until she reached the bottom of the stairs that she thought to look down onto the tracks.

It was the scales she saw first, lining the inner area beneath the opposite platform edge. The creature fit neatly so as not to be squished by the train, its body forming what she had originally assumed was a wall. The scales she had seen the night before as red had turned a cool grey, a result of the chameleon effect she had suspected. The creature would appear as a cement wall to any seer not knowing what to look for.

Seeing the train wouldn't arrive for a few minutes, Lara walked towards one end of the platform. She hoped to find the creature's head, but instead was met with the tail. She stared hard at it, wondering if the dragon, like one she'd known in her childhood, twitched in its sleep like a dog. Minutes later, she didn't hear the train coming, and cried out when it did, passing suddenly before her like a squared, silver version of the beast she was examining.

Casting apologetic glances at the other passengers on the platform, Lara boarded the train quickly. Instead of taking one of the free seats, she moved to the windowed door on the far side of the carriage to get a final look at the dragon as the train left the platform. When the train passed the dragon's head, the creature opened one of its golden eyes, as if it felt her watching. Lara lost her breath, amazed by the startling beauty of the dragon's feline gaze.

At each station that followed, Lara looked eagerly for more dragons. In most she spotted one or more. They were all long and serpentine, their scales grey or black to blend in with their surroundings, but she imagined them as all the colors she knew Chinese dragons to be. Red and blue of the lower caste with their three claws, the various colors of those of higher rank with four claws, and then the rare, top-ranking dragons with their golden scales and five claws, the symbol of the rulers of Ancient China.

Lara's mind buzzed with questions, and an excitement grew inside of her, an old feeling she had not felt since she was a child exploring her family's estate with her father. It wasn't until she unexpectedly heard the announcement for her MRT stop that she realized how far off track her thoughts had gone. Reminded of her looming job interview, she shut her mind off again to the world of the unseen, and made her way off the train towards the busy streets of the city.

* * *

While the sounds of the dragon continued each night, always at 1:45, Lara was able to fight her urge to investigate. She started work the next week, and she was thankful that her life became suddenly busy. Her mornings were booked teaching kindergarten kids and her afternoons, elementary. She got to know her roommates and coworkers and their friends, and did her best to fill her nights with social activities, a luxury she had missed since returning from the Academy three years before.

By late October, Lara's grandmother had given in to email, and shortly after, Skype. The elderly matriarch was surprisingly calm in their first voice conversation, and explained to Lara that a second cousin with a respectable amount of public care-taking experience was watching the family estate temporarily in her absence.

"Now, I understand that you need some time," her grandmother said. "But heed my warning; there is nowhere you can go to avoid who you are as a seer."

"I'm not trying to avoid it, Grandmother," Lara told her. "I just want a break is all. Just before, you know…"

"Being responsible?"

Lara felt heat rise in her cheeks. "That's not fair. Why should I have to be the one—" She stopped herself, her heart racing at what she was about to say.

"Why should you have to be the one to do what, Lara?" her grandmother pressed, bitterness seeping through her words. "No one is forcing you to be a private seer, child, if that's what this is about. You are more than welcome to stay where you are and become a public seer."

"We both know that's not an option for me," Lara muttered.

Lara's grandmother had always made it clear to Lara that her fate was to inherit the family's private seership. Lara knew that to turn away from the job permanently, like her father had done by taking a public seer position years before, would hurt her grandmother. Besides that, Lara was afraid to be a public seer, considering what such hazardous jobs had already done to her family, first taking her grandfather when she was small child, then several years later, her parents. Lara felt trapped, but at the same time, all the more thankful for her decision to leave home, even if it was only for a short time. It gave her space to think about her life on her own terms for once.

"Take a year, Lara. Or two," her grandmother said after a few moments of strained silence. "Or stay," she said, her voice cracking. "I won't fight you on it any more than I fought your father. The choice is yours."

"Grandmother—"

"No, Lara, listen. I don't want you to sit around over there trying to fight who you are. If you do, you'll get bored and find yourself in trouble, child, maybe even falling in with renegade seers."

Lara groaned. "Oh, Grandmother..."

"I'm just warning you of the dangers, child."

"I know, but I'm not bored, Grandmother. Really. I don't even miss the unseen world. At all."

This was the first time Lara had ever lied to her grandmother, something that bothered her long after she got off Skype with her that night. It was true that Lara was happy for the break, but that didn't stop her mind from wandering at times. Just that week she had been on a bus and in her boredom had allowed herself to peek past any potential concealment charms to see if there were any creatures around. Almost right away she had seen a strange bird perched on the side of a building, each of its feathers like a small flame. It was a phoenix, or *fenghuang* in Chinese, and perhaps one of the most dazzling creatures Lara had ever laid eyes on. It had taken every inch of her will power to close her mind again to the unseen world and refocus on the mundane tasks of the day ahead.

To make matters worse, Halloween was approaching, and the teachers at her school had started to put up decorations. The paper bats and plastic pumpkins made it hard for her not to think of the yearly Hallow's Eve events she would soon be missing at her family's estate, or the visitors that would come, magical and human alike, who would be confused and possibly hurt by her disappearance. It was only the feeling of dread that followed such thoughts of home that kept Lara grounded in her decision to stay in Taipei. But that only left her to wonder all the more about her fate, and why she had felt the need to run from something if it was her destiny. Little did she know Fate itself was right around the corner, preparing the events that would answer this question in a most unexpected way.

* * *

It was nearly 2am that night when Lara was woken by the dragon's shrieks. At first she tried to go back to sleep, thinking the creature was enthusiastic in light of the approaching full moon. But when the noise grew even louder, Lara worried that the creature might be upset enough to expose itself to unseeing humans. She wanted to ignore it and leave it to the local seers, but she knew if the Universal Council discovered she had been nearby during the incident and hadn't attempted to help, she would most likely be tried as a renegade seer and possibly have to serve time. Fear spread like ice in the pit of her stomach at the thought, and she moved quickly towards the door.

Her roommate, Hans, was reading on the couch when she stepped into the living room to put on her shoes. "Going to Seven?" he asked, referring to 7-11, the convenient store on nearly every block in Taipei.

"Need anything?" she asked.

"No, but it's late. Do you want me to come with you?"

"I'm ok."

Hans gave her a curious glance from over the couch. "What's so urgent you need it this late?"

"It's an emergency," she said, and then smiled at his raised eyebrows. "You know…" Dragons, magic, she was thinking, but hoped he would think it was a female emergency. He took the bait.

"Right, right," he said. "Well, grab me a Taiwan beer, the bottled kind, if you don't mind."

"Sure. I'll be back soon." She slipped through the door, hoping she would be.

When Lara reached the MRT station five minutes later, the dragon was on the roof, still shrieking and thrashing about. She walked behind the building to a fire ladder she had noticed weeks before. Her heart pounded with a mixture of fear and excitement as she climbed, thinking of what she would say or do once she reached the top. When she stopped at the edge of the roof, she was at the base of the dragon's tail, which moved back and forth like an irritated cat's. She stepped carefully onto the yellow pavilion tiles and cleared her throat.

"Excuse me," she said, hoping that Chinese dragons, like most magical beasts, understood all seers, despite their varying native languages. The dragon turned quickly, bringing its snakelike golden eyes to her face, and blew thick smoke from its nostrils.

"Where's Yin?" it asked, its voice in her head.

"I don't know Yin," she admitted, waving the smoke away. "I'm just here to ask you to quiet down, at least until your seer gets here."

The dragon drew its head back and narrowed its eyes, getting a better look at her. "You're not from here," it said.

"No."

"Where is your land?"

"America," she said.

Smoke came from the dragon's nostrils again and it turned its body around so that it faced her more comfortably. "But you're a seer, aren't you?" it asked.

"Yes, but not... I mean, I'm not a seer here."

A different voice sounded behind Lara. "What are you then?"

It was seer-speak, and even though Lara was aware the words were Chinese, she understood them. She turned and faced whom she assumed to be Yin, dressed in full ninja attire with only his brown eyes showing. "Is that necessary?" she asked. "Coming out here in disguise?"

"It is," he said, "in case anyone were to see me up here at night. Now answer my question. What's a foreign seer doing here? Are you with the Universal Council?"

"I'm just an English teacher."

His eyes narrowed. "Are you a renegade then?"

"No," she said, and blushed. "Nothing like that."

Yin nodded his head and looked at the dragon. "Well, go on, you noisy serpent. I hope your own punish you for your outburst."

"What about you?" the dragon growled. "You're the one who was late."

"I was helping my sister sort out a problem with your brother," Yin said, sounding irritated. "Next time, just be patient. I've never not come, now have I?"

The dragon leapt into the air without another word. It was nearly to the clouds when Yin threw his arms up like Lara had seen him do that first night. The dragon stopped midair and came back down, then launched itself again as soon as it touched the roof.

"Why don't you just let the dragon go?" Lara asked.

"It's a show," Yin explained. "Each night, the dragons of Taipei become visible to all seers in the city. They do this dance and make their noise as a reminder of their role as protectors of the city."

Lara watched as the dragon returned a second time, then a third. On the final time, Yin yelled something Lara didn't quite catch, and when the dragon rocketed into the air, it roared and disappeared into the night sky. Yin then sat down then on the roof tiles and Lara did the same. "So?" he asked, looking at her. "Are you going to explain what you were doing up here with my dragon?"

"Trying to quiet it down before someone unseeing heard."

"The only way for unseeing humans to see or hear a dragon is if the creature wills it," Yin said. "Surely you know that, even as a foreign seer."

"You forget I know nothing about your dragon," she said. "For all I know, it was angry enough to draw attention. It was loud enough to wake me up, and I was sleeping pretty hard."

"Sorry," he said, and then shook his head "I'm not usually late. To be honest, I was done with the problem with my sister's dragon an hour ago, but I got in a fight with my girlfriend." He gave Lara a smile with his eyes. "This job is one of the best seer jobs there is, but some nights I'd like to be a normal person, you know?"

Lara smiled weakly, not sure whether to be happy or discouraged to meet a seer who felt the same way she did.

"My girlfriend isn't a seer," he continued. "So I can't really be honest with her about what I do. She always wants me to stay out partying on Saturday nights." He shrugged. "But I guess that's not honorable anyway, right?" His voice changed to one resembling Finn Flaysen, the president of the Universal Council. "And we seers," he said, "must hold ourselves to a high standard. We are the ones who keep the peace between the world of the seen and unseen. We are the glue that holds two worlds secure."

"The cream in the Oreo," Lara said, and laughed at the surprise that registered in Yin's eyes. "My grandfather used to say that," she told him. "He was killed by an ogre in Russia when I was a kid. An honorable death, our dear president assured us in a letter."

Yin sat up. "I'm sorry to hear that. He was a public seer?"

"Yeah." She paused, biting her lip at the memory of her grandfather's words to her when she had asked him why he wanted to be a public seer when he could live comfortably as a private co-seer with his wife on the family estate. "He took one of the more dangerous jobs, working for the Universal Council. He told me he wanted to make a difference."

"Do you think he did?"

Lara shrugged. "According to the Council he did."

Seeming uneasy with the topic, Yin moved his focus towards the mountains that served as a backdrop in their area of the city. Three red and two blue dragons swarmed together in the distance, resembling ribbons dancing in the wind. "They came from the same litter, those five," Yin said. "They were the first dragons to be born in Taiwan in nearly a hundred years."

"Is that good or bad?" Lara asked.

"It's good more are being hatched, that's for

sure," he said. "But it's sad they are only just now feeling safe enough to grow their population again."

Lara wrapped her fingers around one of the yellow tiles beneath her. "Why are they bound to the stations rather than mountains?"

"They asked for this themselves, actually," Yin said, lying back down on the slanted roof. "It was seers who built the metro tracks, using the dragons' tunnels. The deal was made so they could stay in the stations in the day, and at night, go out to hunt for wild animals in the mountains. It keeps them safe, having the tunnels under seer control and not at risk for anyone else to dig up, and they are close by if they are ever needed to protect the city."

"They don't mind their tunnels being gone?"

"Well they're not. I mean, out here, where the Metro runs above ground, the tunnels don't exist, sure. That's why it's mostly young dragons in these stations. But once you get to Minquan West Road and below, it's all their tunnels. They swarm in those, sometimes even in the day, but they're fast enough to stay out of the way."

"I've seen them sleeping in the stations."

"That's what most do during the day. To be safe." He turned to his side, his eyes brightening with a sudden revelation. "Hey, how long are you here for?"

"I don't know," Lara said. "Why?"

"You familiar with brounies?"

"Sure."

"There's this group of them. You can see them in the streets sometimes if you bother to look, trailing oblivious expats. They're forced to come, you know, being bound to their human families. Anyway, they're having a lot of issues these days. Enough that they've mostly turned to boggarts, and they won't talk to Asian seers about it. They say we don't understand their ways or whatever, which is true."

Lara nodded, trying to suppress her irritation, knowing where the conversation was headed. Brounies were the traditional helpers of many Western households, but when upset for any reason, they quickly turned into trouble-making boggarts. In this more menacing form, they had the potential to cause enough chaos to lead to human conflicts. The issue would have to be dealt with before it escalated. "Isn't there a foreign seer here who can help them?" Lara asked.

"Not right now," Yin said. "We used to have a couple here from England who helped with that sort of thing, but last year they went home. If you're planning on staying here for a while, maybe you can take up their post. Become public seer to the western creatures of Taipei?"

Lara felt her face burn. "No, I don't want a job. I have a job."

"Not a seer job. Which is strange, you know." He studied her through his thick black eyelashes. She wished he would take off his mask so she could see the rest of his face. "Are you sure you aren't part of the renegades?" he asked, his tone teasing. "I hear it starts like this, you know. Trying to avoid seer jobs, refusing to work."

"I'm not refusing to work," Lara said, crossing her arms against the cool breeze coming off the mountains. "I'm just taking a break from my private seership."

She thought Yin was going to ask why, but instead he shrugged, and stuck out his hand. "I'm Yin, by the way."

She took his hand. "I'm Lara."

"It's nice to meet you, Lara," he said, and gave her hand a quick squeeze before releasing it. "Look, tomorrow's Sunday, so I'm assuming you won't be working, right?"

"Right."

"Perfect. The former brounies meet then. Sunday's traditionally their day off, as you probably know. If you're willing to help, even as just as a one-time thing, then I could meet you here at the station at say, 2pm? What do you think?"

Lara sighed. Now that she knew no one was dealing with the problem, she was bound by Universal Law to help. She looked at Yin, sure he must know that, but then found that instead of being angry with him, she was pleased at the thought of interacting with the unseen world again. Even if just once.

"OK," she said, standing. "I'll meet you, but as long as you aren't dressed like that."

"What?" Yin asked looking down at his

outfit. "Oh!" he said, and snatched off his mask, revealing himself as a twenty-something with a five o'clock shadow. "Sorry," he said. "Don't worry, I'll dress normal."

"Great," Lara said, then tilted her head towards the ladder. "I need to get back before my roommates worry, but I'll see you tomorrow. At 2."

"Anything we should bring to the meeting?"

"Yeah," Lara said, fighting her urge to smile. "Lots of milk."

* * *

The boggarts met in an outdoor auditorium at Daan Forest Park in central Taipei. Lara had been to the enormous park before with her new friends for a picnic and to play basketball. It was a lush area, covered in exotic flora and a mixture of modern and traditional Chinese structures. Her favorite feature was the Indian Laurels, which flowed with vines like the Willows at home that hosted some of the friendliest of Dryads.

When Lara and Yin arrived at the auditorium in the park's center, the small elf-like boggarts were already there, growling up a storm with their strange, grumpy form of speech. They glared when they saw the two seers making their way to the top of the concrete bleachers where they sat, but changed their minds about them quickly when they spotted the cartons of milk.

"A gift," Lara told them, and handed them

around. She waited for them to finish, then smiled at their cooling features. They were still boggarts, but a little of their former brounie selves were evident after the offering. "I hear you have problems," she said once she knew it was safe to speak.

"Obviously," one of the larger boggarts said. "We feel unwanted here. Neglected, even. Our humans eat out and hardly bring any food home, and the local creatures have been nothing but rude to us. You'd think our humans would at least leave us out a bowl of milk for our troubles."

"You forget you came uninvited." Lara remarked.

"Did we?" the large boggart said, glowering. "Because last I checked these humans have relied on us their entire lives and—"

"But," Lara said. "They don't even know you exist."

"They hardly have milk," one of the younger boggarts whined. "Even in the cold boxes."

"That's because the milk here isn't real," Lara said.

"It does taste stilted," one boggart said, smacking his lips.

"There are certainly no cows," a female said.

"But we love milk! Real milk!"

"And cream!"

"Look," Lara said, once their voices settled. "The best solution for all of you is to go back to your own lands. As a seer I can release you temporarily from your humans and you can go to your immediate families, or if they're all here, to some relatives. Western foreigners who live here usually only do so for a few years, so chances are your humans will eventually go home and things will go back to normal."

"How do you expect us to get home?" a short, rounded boggart asked.

"The same way you came," Lara said. "In suitcases, carry-ons, coat pockets, whatever. Network. Find out who has humans moving back and when, and go back together, as many as comfortably possible at once."

"But we like to be with our humans…"

"We can't leave them…"

"When my great-grandfather went to war, my father went all the way to--"

"Ok, I know," Lara said, waving her hands. "I get it. But you've turned to boggarts in this state. Either go home and wait for them, or find other ways to deal with your issues so you'll go back to your brounie form. You're only going to cause trouble if you stay this way, and the last thing anyone wants is that, am I right?"

The boggarts blinked their overly large eyes in sync. The largest one stepped forward again. "The Universal Council sent you?"

"No, I'm just here as a favor to Yin."

"The Universal Council tried to send someone from here, but we told them we wouldn't speak to a foreigner. They must have sent you."

"I'm not a public seer. I—"

"A private?" the big boggart asked. "Is your territory here?"

"No, it's—"

"Because if you're a seer with no job or territory, maybe you can stick around and help us. You know, the brounies and other expat creatures of Taipei."

"We really could use you," Yin said. "There's this group of Irish fairies up on Maokong Mountain who came over when—"

"No, no, no," Lara said, her face flushed. "Look, I came here for a break from my seership, not to—" She stopped, seeing the startled looks on the boggarts' faces. "I'm sorry," she said. "It's just," she turned to Yin. "Like you said last night, sometimes it would be nice to be normal."

"If you want to be normal, can't you do something bad and lose your sight?" a tiny boggart child asked.

"No, I'd be tried as a renegade and most likely locked up."

"Or killed," the big boggart said, crossing his arms with a smug look on his face. "Look, Madame Seer, this is how I see it. You're here, you want a break from your own affairs, fine. But we'll need help with our issues if we choose to stay, or help to be released if we don't. And it's not just us with problems, but some other expat creatures as well. Now that we know you're here, word will spread. You'll be sought out. You can either agree to help us, or go home."

Lara sighed. "I hear Japan is nice."

"Japan's got its own expat problems," Yin said. "The boggart's right."

"Hey!" the boggart said, offended by the term brounies viewed as derogatory.

"Sorry," Yin said. "The brounie here is right, Lara. It doesn't matter where in the world you go, you are what you are. You can't hide from that."

Feeling defeated, Lara sunk down onto one of the bleachers. As she did, one of the boggart children, still in almost a brounie state, jumped into her lap. "Do you hate helping us?" it asked.

"No," Lara said, placing a hand on the boggart child's back. "It's not that at all. I like being a seer."

"Then why are you trying not to be one?" the boggart child asked.

Lara pursed her lips. It was the first time anyone had thought to actually ask her that question directly. "I was bored," she said, then relaxed at the confession. "I was a private seer on my family's estate, one of the only humans around."

"You got no family?" one of the boggarts asked near her feet.

"None that live with me anymore."

"Don't you want to get married and have seer babies?" the boggart child asked from her lap.

"Maybe, one day," Lara said. "But for now, it's nice to be around other people every day, and I can't do that as a private seer. At least not on my family's estate."

"But you could as a public seer, right?" one of the women boggarts asked.

"Especially in a city this large," Yin said. "You'd get all sorts of perks if you took the job. I mean, surely your family wouldn't mind if you took to public service, especially if that's what your grandfather did."

"And my parents," Lara said. "But that's the problem. My grandfather died as a public seer and my parents went missing years ago on some expedition in Greenland. I'm not too sure I want to go into the same line of work as them. What if my family is cursed or—" Lara stopped talking, seeing the strange look on Yin's face. "What'd I say?" she asked.

"Your parents disappeared in Greenland?" he asked.

"Yeah. Why?"

"They disappeared together?" he asked, speaking slowly. "As public seers?"

"Yes, but that was years ago, when I was just a kid."

Yin's expression softened. "Was it in 1999?"

Lara blinked. "How do you know that?"

"I didn't," he said. "I just thought, well... My dad disappeared in Greenland in 1999, along with an American couple, Hank and Bonnie, and I thought... that can't be a coincidence, can it?"

"No," Lara said. "No, not at all. Those were my parents."

Yin nodded, looking pale. "I'd heard they had a daughter. I just never thought…I mean, I never thought I'd meet you."

Lara felt a chill, as if Fate itself had released its icy breath, betraying its presence in their mist. What were the odds, she thought, that of all seers she could have met in Taiwan, of all seers she could have met in the world, she would meet the very one whose father had been with her parents on the Greenland expedition. She hadn't even realized that the man with her parents had been Taiwanese. She'd never allowed herself to dig that deep for fear of what she'd find. Or wouldn't.

"Without a trace," she said, pulled back to the memory of the telegram that had arrived. "My grandmother spent a year in Greenland after that, trying to find them."

"Many people tried," Yin said.

The boggarts were silent now, watching them through wide eyes, their expressions curious at the tense exchange before them.

"Have you ever thought of going to Greenland to investigate?" Yin asked.

Lara shook her head. "When my grandmother returned, she told me the site had been closed off to seers and humans alike."

"That's close to the truth," Yin said. "It's closed off to seers without at least seven years of experience in seer service. I have three under my belt now. How many did you manage before running off here?"

"Three."

"Well," Yin said. "As I see it, you should stick around here with me and my sister, Wei Wei. We plan to go to Greenland and figure out what happened as soon as we can. She's got one year of service on me, but she'd gladly wait for us to catch up."

Lara sat in place, allowing excitement to fill her just for a moment before she reminded herself of the reality of her fate. There was no way, she felt sure, she could neglect her family's seership for the four years and beyond it would take to accomplish what Yin was proposing. Even if she returned to her job until she had her seven years of experience, she could never walk away again, not at the risk of causing more damage to her relationships with the creatures in her seership. But then, how could she not at least consider Yin's offer when it was so clear Fate had directed the crossing of their paths?

"I need some time to think about this," she told Yin, but what she needed to do was talk to Betty. She hadn't called the estate, not once since arriving in Taipei months before, too scared of the state in which she'd find the world she had abandoned, and certain the phone call would result in her being begged to return home. Now she knew she had to take that risk. She had to see if Fate was indeed leading her down this strange new path, or if she should stop hiding and accept her life as a private seer.

"Take your time, Lara," Yin said, then

smiled. "But not too much if you want to come with Wei Wei and me. I'm not nearly as patient as she is."

Feeling sick with anxiety, Lara placed the boggart child on the bench next to her and stood, facing the boggarts one last time. "It was lovely to meet you today, friends. I wish you the best, whether we meet again or not, and I hope you consider my counsel."

They gave her a slight bow, and she could see their features had softened even more. When she turned to leave, she waved goodbye to Yin before he could follow, not wanting him to see the emotions at war inside of her as she wrestled with the question of her fate.

* * *

Lara used Skype to call her family estate as soon as the sun was up on the East Coast.

"Oh, Lara, it's so lovely to hear from you!" Betty said. "How's Taiwan? Tell me everything."

"It's great, Betty, really," Lara told her, feeling as if a ball of lead were sitting in the pit of her stomach. "I've met another seer here, and he had me meet with some boggarts earlier today."

"Boggarts? In Taiwan? Well, I hope you were able to help them."

"Yes, well, apparently there're quite a few expat creatures here in need of a seer. They prefer someone more familiar with their customs."

"Sounds like a good job for you!" Betty said.

"I knew you'd find use for your skills there."

Lara felt the weight in her stomach lift. "So you aren't upset that I'm gone?" she asked.

"No, no," Betty said cheerfully. "We all miss you, of course, but Mathilda is handling things well enough. I think she'd be happy to take this job long-term, if you decide to stay where you are for now."

"I'm considering it," Lara said, relief flooding through her. "I like it here."

"Well, good," Betty said. "But be sure to visit us when you can. Everyone misses you. We have our Hallow's Eve event in two weeks. I wish you could come!"

"Me too," Lara said.

"They have dragons there, don't they?"

"Sure. I met one yesterday, actually."

"Oh, good. You must make friends with it. You remember, don't you? That's how your parents used to visit us when they went on their assignments abroad. By dragon! They said the creatures cut the journey time down so it seemed more a taxi ride than a flight. I don't know how public seer jobs are now, but back then, the option to borrow a dragon for vacation was one of the perks of the job."

Lara walked to the window. It was still early, but she knew Yin's dragon was sleeping in the station a five-minute walk away. She wondered what it and Yin would think of a Halloween trip to her family estate, and how easy it would be for them to get permission once she accepted the public seer job, as she now knew she would.

She saw it all then, in a flash, what could be. In the four years of public service in Taiwan, she and Yin, and his sister, Wei Wei, could begin investigating on their own, to pave the way for what they would be allowed to do once their seven years of service were complete. It all made sense then, the boredom she had felt at home, yet her desire to be a seer. She had been too much of a coward to consider a fate outside of what she had been raised to accept, so Fate itself had driven her from home to the very place she needed to be to join forces with Yin and Wei Wei for the future that awaited them. They would make it to Greenland, she felt certain. They would find out what happened to their parents, whether good or bad. Then, perhaps, there would be more. A life of excitement. A life of adventure. It's what she had wanted, despite her fears, despite how it would hurt her grandmother. Fate's hand had led her right where she needed to be.

"You know, Betty," Lara said, turning away from the window. "I just might be able to manage a quick trip home." And for the first time in weeks, the dread of going home was gone, replaced with warmth and peace. "I'll see if I can be there for Hallow's Eve, ok?"

About the Author

L.L. Phelps grew up in the American South, with a few years on a Montana ranch. Since graduating college, she has lived on three continents, and hopes to at least visit a few more. For now she lives in Taipei with her husband, two dogs, and a fridge-top sleeping cat named Thor. She is currently working on a multitude of speculative fiction short stories, and a few non-speculative projects under the pseudonym, Ellyna Ford Phelps. You can follow her on twitter @LLPhelps1.

Bitter Pill

by
Katrina A. Brown

Most people in Keelung were watching the news when the alarm sounded. It was, after all, 6pm, when family, friends or strangers gathered at home or at a neighborhood restaurant, to digest dinner and catch up on the day's events. News in Keelung was almost another dish on the table, necessary to complete the meal, and televisions were part of every restaurant's furniture. All stations were running stories around the same theme; overpopulation of the region and what to do about it. "News of the day" for so long now, viewers did not bother discussing it.

Television stations each took the sides of their sponsoring political parties. The opposition-sponsored television stations suggested that those in power now might like to take their followers and find peace down the south of the island. Stations supported by the governing political party encouraged the opposition and its supporters to move out through one of the many tunnels or over one of the larger bridges, and find a new start away from the grime, crime, and corruption they so often denounced the party for causing. And they all asked the same question: What was the mayor doing about it? The mayor's grunts and sighs of non-committal seemed to get him through every debate unscathed.

This particular evening's version of the news was interrupted by the piercing one second ring, two second whirr, and one second break pattern ringing from the Civil Defense speakers on the hilltops and in alleyways, along rivers and ocean walkways. The people of Keelung were used to the sounds of sirens. In this geographically-tiny city of almost a million, hardly a minute went by when there wasn't an ambulance, fire engine, or police car rushing down a stinking, crowded street. The usual reaction was to ignore them, and people did just that, calmly eating their noodles, rice, chicken fat. But the sound continued. It could not be ignored. People put down their bamboo chopsticks and paper cups, and craned their necks to see the subtitles on the television screens.

"The siren at Kuo-Sheng Power Plant has sounded." The formality of the name of the nuclear power facility just 25 kilometers from central Keelung struck at least one person in Pei-Ling Lin's noodle shop as funny. "Kuo-Sheng? Why not call it what we all know it as? It's Number Two, just Number Two." The announcer of course, could not hear this quip, and continued to mouth his speech. Pei-Ling turned from her metal cart where she was preparing noodles, soup, and vegetables for her customers. She wiped the sweat off her forehead with a microfiber cloth, wiped her hands on her polyester apron, and went to turn the television up.

Pei-Ling ran the noodle shop to help support her two children's extra-curricular activities. She usually was not there so late, but her waitress had called in sick at the last minute, so she had messaged her children and stayed on for the dinner rush. Her children were now home, and even though they were old enough to be there for a little while, they could not be left alone during a crisis. She had to know what was going on.

Customers eating in Pei-Ling's noodle shop were glued to their metal stools, staring at the television hanging on the wall above one of the eight formica-top tables. All conversation had stopped. The only sounds Pei-Ling could hear were the whirring of the industrial fan on the other side of the small room, the television news reporter, and the intermittent siren calling from just down the street. Pei-Ling crossed the room and pulled the greasy string of the fan to turn it off. It would soon be stifling, but at least everyone in the shop could hear the television clearly.

"Residents are advised to return home and find the container handed out by the government after the Fukishima Disaster in 2011. It has a date stamp on the box. It looks like this." The shaky hand of the youthful-looking newsreader held a clear plastic box by its handle. It was about the size of cardboard tissue box, and had the words "A gift from the Keelung Government" written in red Chinese characters across the side facing the viewer. The newsreader put the container down and opened the lid. He pulled out a white oblong cardboard box, just big enough to fit a lighter inside. It was totally free of text or images. It was just an innocent little box. "You need to open up this box right up and then open the first metal wrapper on the pill, like this. Follow the instructions that are inside. Stay safe and goodnight."

* * *

Realization was a great hypnotist. Those eating out simply stood up, collected their belongings and left. Customers forgot to pay, and staff forgot to collect payment. Families at home looked at each other across their Lazy Susans, completely forgetting to thank grandma for the freshly picked and fried bean sprouts. This was not a drill. There was something wrong with nuclear reactor No. 2. The government had prepared for this and now the people of Keelung needed to find out what they had to do to stay alive. Pei-Ling took a deep breath and scanned her empty shop. The dishes could wait. She had to get home and find that box.

Nobody noticed the fight breaking out in the newsroom of Channel 56. The trembling newsreader that had made the emergency announcement now clutched the pill and the white box with a two-handed fist against his chest. The two young weather girls clambered over him, one hitting him with her high heel shoe, the other scratching at his hands with well-manicured nails. He clutched these small items until his knuckles bled and his head and shoulders pounded. When he could not hold onto the treasure any longer, he threw it up into the air for the two girls to fight over as he ducked out between them and ran free.

* * *

The siren was still ringing, now with breaks of three minutes between assaults. Mr. Chen, the long-standing Mayor of Keelung, sat in his enormous chair carved from the wood of a banyan tree. On the wall facing him was a large map of the area he resided over. He knew the statistics. Population 900,429. Geographical area 132.7589 square kilometers. 95% hills. His mayorship of this region was not without its challenges.

Mayor Chen's eyes reverted to the mass of newspaper clippings on the desk. Headlines focused on his great headache. Exactly who should be moved out of this North-Eastern part of Taiwan? Should they expel the migrant workers, Mainland Chinese families, and foreign spouses – all conveniently grouped under the welcoming flag "New Immigrants"? Statistics proved that the women in these categories were having more children than local parents, ignoring the warnings from the government and general public about constant food shortages, lack of housing, and pressure on sanitation services. Maybe they should relocate the 250,000 refugees that had moved in after Taipei's devastating earthquake in 2016. Infrastructure had not improved since 2010, when it was already at what many considered its overload point of serving 387,000 residents. Keelung's population was now at over 900,000. It was a pimple on the back of the Taiwan Central Government, who were scared to squeeze it in case of infection.

Mayor Chen shook his shoulders and drew in a nasally snort. He had to leave his office before the first visitors and phone calls, or there would be no escape. Just like the population crisis, he had no control over the nuclear disaster plan. Resources had come from Central Government, as had the directive, even if it was sent out under the guise of his Local Government: To each household with members of reproducing age, deliver one little anti-radiation pill, in one little white box. These kits had been distributed right after the 2011 Fukushima

Disaster. Families had politely accepted the first-aid kits, and he imagined, simply put them next to their own existing ones without a second look. Certainly, nobody had mentioned the fact that each household had received only one iodine pill.

Chen was thankful he had been smart enough to take a first-aid kit for himself and hide it at the Mayoral address, as soon as he had caught wind of the Central Government's plan. This gave him his very own little box of survival, before it was designated to another household. It reminded him of playing the local version of Monopoly with his son, when he had stolen one of the boy's "Get Out of Keelung Free" cards. Just like the game, he had a pill for his son, and a pill for himself.

It was a pity about his wife, but they had had 16 good years, and she had always smiled when she told him, "A woman's role in a family is to suffer." He would not be going home to watch her say goodbye to their son. He could imagine her, packing up a healthy snack box and a flask of warm soup, adding extra socks to the boy's backpack, and kissing him on the forehead. He would send his wife a text, tell her he was ordered to remain at his post, and that he would come home tomorrow to be with her. He hoped her death would be painless. More importantly, he hoped that she would not live long enough to realize his desertion. She was a good woman, a realistic woman, so he knew she would accept it, but he would, of course, rather be remembered by her as the loyal husband he had tried his best to present to her.

Mayor Chen took a long look at the map. Right at its edge was the Taipei to Yilan Hsue-Shan Tunnel. Completed in 2006, the tunnel was 12.9 kilometers long, and stretched over six major fault-lines and thirty-six high-pressure groundwater sources. Dramas had included a Japanese engineer threatening to commit *hari-kari* if they continued the dangerous excavation, and 25 accidental deaths over the 15 years of construction. Earlier this year, the two-laned East-bound tunnel had been closed by Central Government for several weeks for its 20-year servicing. An enormous wooden barricade had been made to cover the exit. On Mayor Chen's last trip back from Yilan, the barricade had reminded him of a door to a giant dungeon. Now it would be the route for the chosen escapees from the nuclear disaster area.

Remembering the need to text his wife, Chen searched the surface of his antique red cypress desk for his phone. Finally finding it under some papers, he picked it up and looked out the window while he formulated the message in his head. It was starting to rain.

* * *

"Mama, Mama, open the box! Mama open the box!" Pei-Ling's children chanted, an uncharacteristic edge of tension in their voices as they bounced on their bottoms on Pei-Ling's bed, trying to get a better look at the box. It was very small, even in Pei-Ling's hands. Pei-Ling was taken back to a time when her house had been spacious, when she had sat at the window sill and her husband had taken a photograph of her; her delicate hands on the window's ledge, her almond-shaped eyes looking out across the wide street. She, and her house, had been beautiful then. Soon after the photograph, their home had been divided in two by government mandate, to accommodate a family of refugees from Taipei City. That lovely wide street had later been split into two streets, and if she put her still-slender fingers out that window now, she could actually touch the neighbor's security bars.

"The box!" Her children's voices brought her back to her little room, where the "wall cancer" was already attacking the concrete, forcing the paint to bubble and chip off in palm-sized pieces. Squashing her thoughts of romantic days past, Pei-Ling tore open the foil package and unfolded the paper stashed inside. A note was typed up in small font, with two numbers written in red ink at the bottom.

This pill is for one member of your household. It is not to be taken until the instruction is given on-board the evacuation buses that will leave at 3am the morning after the nuclear disaster siren sounds. The buses will leave from Keelung Harbour entrance, outside Keelung Train Station and head to Yilan County. Bring this piece of paper to the meeting point. The two numbers below are your bus and seat allocation. Every barcode is unique. Forgery is punishable by death. To those staying in the radiation zone, be reassured your names will live on in the heart and soul of the people you let go forth into the future.

"That's it?" Hao-Ping turned the page over and made sure there was nothing on the other side of the paper. There wasn't.

"What does it mean, Mama?" Mei-Mei asked, eyes wide with confusion. "Are we going to die?" Pei-Ling looked out that window again, trying to find the words to reassure her children. What was she to do? Her husband was driving a tour bus up through the central mountain ranges, and would have not have telephone reception until tomorrow. Tomorrow would be far too late. One of them was going to take that pill and one of them was going to die with their mother.

Pei-Ling moved over to sit on the bed between her children. Mei-Mei was begging to her big brother, Hao-Ping.

"Please, give it to me. I don't want to stay, Ge-Ge."

"Maybe it won't be so bad. Maybe nothing will happen. Oh! Mei-Mei, I'm so sorry for our fights. You have to give me the pill. It is going to be scary, away from Mama and Baba. I'll make sure your memory lives on." Hao-Ping had a slight whine in his voice, as if choking back his own fear.

"Ge-Ge! I want to swallow it now." Mei-Mei was getting agitated.

"It's not time. Be brave. Give it to me. Maybe we'll all live anyway and will be back in a day or two to fight over Mama's desserts again."

Pei-Ling wiped her eyes with the handkerchief. Looking at the music awards she had taped to the bare concrete spots along the wall, she thought of the plans she had for her babies – graduation, marriage, parenthood – and how they were crumbling fast around her. What could she do? How could she conjure up another pill and make sure her children could at least take care of each other after she was gone?

It was hot. Was the radiation already leaking into their very home? She had to try something. She would go and call on the neighbors. They were reaching their twilight years, and always treated her children well. Blinking back tears, Pei-Ling knocked gently on the bedroom door.

"Children, I am going to see the Lee's for a few minutes. Please give me the box you are holding and I will look after it for you." Her children looked up at her from the bed. Hao-ping was looking more like her husband everyday. He was supposed to be attending High School in the fall. His little sister was eagerly awaiting the first signs of puberty, and still needed her Mama to sleep with her at night. She felt her heart would wrench itself out of her body right at that moment, but she had to think, to stay composed. She touched each of them lightly on the shoulder, then took the box and put it in her skirt pocket.

"Wait here, I'll be back."

* * *

Shaking her head at the rain, she took an umbrella from the stand by the door. How much longer would she be able to do that? When would the radiation start to affect her body? So far, the air outside felt normal; it was her heart that was tragically heavy. She wiped away another tear and headed next door.

Pei-Ling didn't have to knock. The elderly couple was sitting outside under the awning of their open doorway, on the little wooden school chairs that had been there since Pei-Ling had first moved into the area with her husband. Grandma Lee had her skirt lifted up around over her knees. She was using the extra material as a fan.

"Oh, hello, Pei-Ling. It really is hot and damp, isn't it? Rain isn't helping things, either."

"Yes, it is, Mrs. Lee –"

"Dear, I know why you are here. If I had a pill, I would give it to you. I can't stand this heat. I guess it is going to get a lot hotter." Mrs. Lee hacked a long, wheezy cough. "But I think we were too old to be considered for the pill, even back when it was handed out. How long ago was that, now?"

"Ten years." Pei-Ling tried to stay composed.

"Now, now." Kindly old Mr. Lee reached over and patted Pei-Ling's arm. He turned momentarily to spit out a watermelon seed shell. "Whoever you save, they will light incense in your memory, you can be sure of that. It might just be earlier than you had hoped for, that's all."

"Yes, death comes to us all." Mrs. Lee smiled a wise smile. "Let's brave it out together."

Pei-Ling sucked in her lips and picked up her umbrella. What was in that rain, she wondered. The siren started up again. Now it was going off only every forty minutes. Why was it forty minutes? Was it someone's bad joke, reminding the population of the innocent times of elementary school, when the bell would ring every forty minutes and students would come out the doors like bees from a hive in Spring? Who was she going to send away from this disaster area, and who was she going to keep beside her, to die with her right here in this damp, hot, overcrowded city that was usually full of high spirits and laughter despite the lack of food and housing? With a weight like uranium in her heart, she took her small, quick steps back to her children.

* * *

"Come and eat some dumplings," Pei-Ling called from the tiny living room. Not sure if the nausea was from fallout or heartbreak, she had still managed to cook a simple dinner. After putting food on the two plates on the table in front of her treasured Hao-Ping and Mei-Mei, she fell into a chair herself. How were these words going to come out?

Unable to look at the two innocent faces watching her every emotion, Pei-Ling started her speech.

"Hao-Ping, Mei-Mei." She took their hands in hers. "You are everything I always wanted and more. Hao-Ping, you are your father's pride as well as the first son of the first son. Baba would want you to carry on the prayers for past generations. Mei-Mei, I need you to be with me. I can't put you on that bus alone. What might happen to you–"

"No! No!" Mei-Mei screamed in realization. "I don't want to die! I don't! I don't!" Her heart-wrenching cries faded as she collapsed into Pei-Ling's lap.

"Am I going...alone?" Fear was apparent in Hao-Ping's voice.

"Not all alone, son." With shaking hands, Pei-Ling opened Hao-ping's palm and placed the pill and red bag of coins inside. "These are the last of the lucky coins from grandma's funeral. I promise they will always keep you safe and successful."

Gently removing Mei-Mei from her lap, Pei-Ling stood up and straightened her skirt.

"Oh, my dear, first-born child. Let's get you packed."

* * *

Around the tiny curved road outlining Keelung Harbor, one thousand tour buses were lined up, backed up, and squashed up in a chaotic order that residents were used to. Forty thousand passengers were being seen off by their family and friends, but the scene was calm. It was like a morning at the wet market, but people were comparing bus numbers rather than fish prices. Young Army recruits stood holding T98s, the locally-produced pride of the Taiwan Military, nervously across their chests. They had been told to be ready to control the crowd. In return, there were two buses dedicated to taking them out of the area, and they had been gifted full-face gas-masks designed to prevent inhalation of nuclear particles.

Pei-Ling and her children were standing at the outer edge of the huge crowd. As she handed her jade necklace to her brother, Mei-Mei whispered, "I don't need this anymore." Hao-Ping wrapped his fingers over the curved piece of opaque green stone. Shaped like an inverted rainbow, with four characters engraved on the arch, it promised the wearer longevity and health. Pei-Ling remembered knotting the cotton chain. She thought her heart would burst. Yet, like those thousands of people around her, she followed the cultural rules and remained stoic.

"Here is your breakfast and lunch, and some extra crackers for you to share with your neighbor. I have hidden some cans of peanut soup in your socks in your backpack. Oh, my son, I hope you don't go hungry! Your father's number is in my cellphone. I have put that in your bag, too. Make sure you call him once you know where you are going."

Hao-Ping could not make any sound come

out of his mouth. He leaned into his mother. She held him close and tight. "Away you go then. Come back and light incense for us one day." Hao-Ping stepped back. Keeping his head down, he felt his breast pocket, making sure the little white box with his pill was still there. It was. It was time to go.

* * *

Mayor Chen stood in the middle of the crowd gathering in front of the buses. His cap was pulled down as far has he could get it. As long he kept his shoulders hunched over and head down, he would be hard to recognize. It was too bad he had forgotten to wear a surgical mask. The air was rancid. With the reactor shut down, Keelung was effectively suffering a brown-out. Electricity was just making it to homes. Most air conditioners were not working. Street lamps were running at half-light. Neon signs now dimmed, and for the first time in generations, people could see the stars from within the city. Humidity was high and even with the sea breeze attempting to flow in from the harbor, the air was thick and damp. Mayor Chen could feel the particles of grime begin to cling to his arms. He wished he had worn a long-sleeved shirt to his office. This shirt was the last one his wife would iron for him. How long would it take her to die? Some people had started to develop initial symptoms of radiation poisoning, declaring themselves nauseous and feverish, even throwing up. People knew from media reports during the 2011 Fukishima Disaster that they would suffer these conditions as soon as a few hours after being exposed to radiation from the damaged reactor. He thought of the text she had sent reminding him to eat well and drink more water. An answer was unnecessary. She would be satisfied with her sacrifice for the men in her family.

Feeling in his shirt pocket, Mayor Chen found the little white box. He opened up the sealed silver package and took a long look at the paper inside. He peered over at the paper of a young woman beside him. Her piece of paper was covered in printed text, and had two numbers printed on it. His sheet had instructions, but no numbers or barcode. How did he miss getting a seat allocation? Chen squinted to see the number on the bus closest to him. He took a blue fine-point marker from his pocket and carefully traced in the characters *Bus two. Seat two.* That should do the trick. Making sure the white pill was safe in the box, he slipped the paper back inside and strolled toward the bus.

Bus number two was one of the newest vehicles in the line. Luggage was being placed in the bottom compartment. Passengers would sit high up on the second level, so they could enjoy the view on their journey. For many, this would be their first trip out of this area. However, this did not feel like a vacation. Tension ran through the crowd. They were in front of the old bank that had been bombed during World War II. Now, like their ancestors, they were refugees. This time, they were victims of peace and prosperity.

"Ba! Ba!" A face and then arms, and then a whole body, clung to Mayor Chen. Putting his hands on his son's shoulders, the mayor gently pushed the teenager away from him. Chen contorted his mouth into pouting, grinning, and then frowning expressions, in an attempt to alert the boy to the fact he was bringing unwanted attention to the two of them. His son stood quietly for a moment, and then asked, "Are you here to see me off?

Chen coughed. "I'm going with you. As Mayor, I have to go."

"Oh, thank goodness, I won't be alone afterall. How will I find you once we reach our destination? What bus are you on?" His son asked.

"Eh, bus two. Seat two." Chen held up his forged paper.

"Me, too! Right next to me, too!" Excitement rushed out of his son, as he waved his genuine sheet, with "Seat four" printed on it. That was a window seat.

The vein in the mayor's forehead twitched. "What a coincidence. We'll have a fun ride together."

"C'mon Ba, you did an awesome job, getting us a seat together! Let's get on the bus."

* * *

Hao-Ping looked at his paper and then at the buses in front of him. Bus number eight was in front of him, number nine was behind. Bus number two must be in front, then. He could see from the blue and white circular logo and spray-painted image of the spectacular Jade Mountain that it belonged to his dad's new company. He wondered where his father was. Did he know of the tragedy unfolding around his family? It would break his heart, Hao-Ping knew. With the innocent pride of a young soldier going to war, he felt the responsibility of saving his family's legacy from this disaster. He would finish high school, marry a girl from the South, and settle down somewhere safe, perhaps even immigrate.

The flow of the moving crowd brought Hao-Ping back to the present. Craning his neck, he tried to pick out familiar faces in the sea of damp bodies and umbrellas. He hadn't had time to contact any of his classmates to see whether they were getting the tickets out. The crowd was mostly made up of young men, so it was likely there were people he knew here, but he could not see in this jumble. Giving up on his search, he took his rack sack up onto the top level of the bus he had finally reached. Seat two, his ticket showed. There was a soft middle-aged man sitting in that seat. Hao-Ping took a deep breath. Trying to be at once polite and self-assured, he said to the man in front of him, "Excuse me. You are in my seat."

The man did not look up. "Uh, no, this is my

seat. Look." He took a paper out of his hands and held it up with his sweaty thumbs. "Bus two, seat two. This young man will tell you I have the original ticket. It's just that my bar code was torn off. See, here?" The mayor held up the newly-torn corner of his ticket, to show where the bar code should have been.

Hao-Ping rubbed his nose with the back of his right hand.

"I'm sorry, Sir. This is my seat. Look here. I have a bar code on my ticket." He held it up for the man to see.

"Let me get a closer look." Mayor Chen snatched the ticket. "Oops! Now both of our tickets are torn." Mayor Chen pulled Hao-Ping's shirt front, forcing Hao-Ping's face so close to his that Hao-Ping could smell the garlic and dumpling remains of the man's dinner. Mayor Chen whispered intimately, "The military police won't know whose bar code it is. One of us will be shot, it says so in the instructions. Let's see if we can share this seat. The three of us can sit together. It could be fun. We can play hide-the-body. This is my son Xiao-Hei. You can call me Shi-Jang."

Hao-Ping looked around the bus. All the seats were taken. Everyone was conspicuously staring out their windows, pretending to ignore the minor scene he was making. Seeing no way out, he put his ruck sack at his feet and let "Shi-Jang" squeeze him in between father and son. The seats were plush and he usually sank into them, but now the rise of the edges of the two seats squashed into the crack of his buttocks. He did not dare complain.

Without warning, a military police officer appeared on the steps of the bus. The mayor moved quickly, squashing Hao-Ping behind him. Hao-Ping's ribs were squashing into his lungs. He tried desperately not to gasp. Mayor Chen turned his body toward the military police officer and held up a ticket, hoping the bar code looked attached. The officer's vision was obscured by his gas mask. He took a cursory glance around, turned, and stepped off the bus. Hao-Ping could not believe "Shi-Jang" had gotten away with that so easily. "Shi-Jang" moved over, giving him room enough to look out the window, over Xiao-Hei's quiet form in the window-seat. Hao-Ping could see tears forming in the boy's eyes. He wondered why "Shi-Jang" didn't sit in the middle and comfort his son.

Bus number one was now doing a large U-turn, back to the narrow overpass that led to the entrance of Highway 3. Their bus driver started the engine and followed the older bus in front. As they drove up on the ramp, Hao-Ping watched the pollution-gray concrete mish-mash of buildings slowly disappear behind them. As they drove out of Keelung and into New Taipei County, the green ferns and low-lying vegetation of the hills filled the large windows. Hao-Ping could feel his left arm already going numb as it was pushed under the weight of "Shi-Jang". That man looked very familiar, but he couldn't quite place him. With his free arm, Hao-Ping felt his chest pocket again. The pill box was still there. There was a little booklet from his mother. He took it out and opened it to the first page.

* * *

The mayor could read all the signs on the back of bus number one. The coaches formed a long winding serpent on the mountain highway. On either side of them were the jagged mountain ranges that blocked out the view of the sea. In front of them was the newly-upgraded tunnel. They would be honored with being the first group to go through the South-bound tunnel. Only one lane was open to traffic, meaning the buses would line up as if racing to the ocean. He could imagine that moment when they would come out of the mouth of the tunnel and see the gorgeous blues and greens of sea and farmland. The concrete blocking the entrance during construction would be gone, of course. He looked at his sleeping son, then at the boy squeezed in next to him. The boy was reading a little book. Curious, he leaned over to see what it was.

Hao-Ping looked up and said, "My mom gave me this copy of Di Zi Gui. She hopes I can grow up to be a responsible, caring man. Do you remember reading it when you were in school?"

A line popped out at Mayor Chen:

When parents fall ill, one tastes the medicine first (to see if it's been brewed to the proper degree).

"I do, I do." Said the Mayor, a wry smile on his face.

* * *

The bus was cruising at a steady 70 kilometers an hour. At this speed, the turns on the local highway were quite smooth. It was very quiet. The sporadic release of a weep or cough reminded Mayor Chen that some passengers had said goodbye to people they truly loved. He was wondering how that might feel when an image of their president appeared on the bus' karaoke screen. The president's square head took up most of the screen. His graying hair was flicked to one side, and clung to his head, wet with either hair wax or sweat. His mouth was saying words of courage, his eyes were customarily blank.

"You have been chosen to represent the future of Keelung. Your temporary move will ensure it grows and prospers as it was meant to upon your return. Feel glad. You will be remembered. Your government will make sure your loved ones do not suffer. Now, take your pill, sit back, and enjoy the ride through the pride of Taiwan, our newly-renovated Yilan Tunnel."

A typed note replaced the president's head. Reading the simple instruction, passengers obediently opened the little boxes, and popped open the foil. Hao-Ping and Xiao-Hei looked at the Mayor. They copied him as he opened the box. The pill was white like the box. It was void of any grooves or markings. So innocent. Just a little pill. It was hard to imagine they had been so lucky as to get this chance at living. The three of them put their pills in their mouths. The two boys had water bottles, and they used that water to wash the pills down. Xiao-Hei offered the bottle to his father, but Mayor Chen refused, wriggling his closed mouth and pointing to his neck, indicating he had already swallowed the little white pill. Bus by bus, the mouth of the Hsue-Shan Tunnel swallowed them up.

* * *

It was a slow ride through the tunnel. And uncharacteristically dark. On past trips for government business, the tunnel had been bright and filled with the regular echo of a recording; a woman's voice asking travelers to tune their radios to the traffic station. There was no cellphone reception and no other radio service in the tunnel. Mayor Chen thought of the facts he knew about the craggy mountain range that sat right on top of them. 54 peaks were over 3,000 meters high. Hsue-Shan Peak was the tallest of them all. Of these, 19 were in the "Top 100 Peaks of Taiwan" that mountaineers aspired to conquer. With no such desire himself, he was happy to sit on this bus and wait for the magical moment when the early morning glow of sunlight would glow from the tunnel exit.

* * *

The mayor looked around him. Everyone was asleep. It must be the effects of the pill. He took the white pill from his own palm and blew it dry before putting back into the box. That line about letting the young try the medicine first had saved him from this deep sleep. The mayor tapped his son on the shoulder. The boy's glasses had slipped down his nose a little, and tiny bubbles of spittle were forming around his mouth.

Suddenly, the bus came to a halt. A minute later, the bus driver walked up the stairs and looked around the bus. Seeming satisfied, he said a quiet "A *mi tuo* fo" and then unwrapped his little pill from the surrounding foil. The mayor coughed.

"What's going on? Why is everyone asleep?"

The bus driver looked at him with surprise. "It's the directive. We take the pill and go to sleep. The pill will keep us safe from radiation while we wait here. Then when we wake up, we wait for directions, and head on to our new lives."

"And you're going to do that?"

"There's nothing else to do. Our government wouldn't harm its people." The driver studied Chen for a moment. I know you. You are our mayor. What are you doing here?"

"Eh..."

"Aren't you supposed to be back in Keelung, keeping order? We were told you'd be there to look after our families. Why are there three of you on the seat?"

"I'll be going back after things settle. Need to be healthy to help."

The driver looked at him through narrowed eyes, "Are you sure?"

Mayor Chen watched the driver slowly turn and head down to his seat on the lower level of the bus.

* * *

Back in Keelung, the sun was rising. The sirens had stopped their song. In pockets of hills above the quiet harbor, the mournful chanting of monks could be heard. Pei-Ling and her daughter Mei-Mei were inside the small temple near their home. Like everyone else gathered in the safety of the temple, they were dressed in everyday clothes, as was the tradition for death preparation. Pei-Ling lovingly patted the cool stone carvings in the columns that held up the roof. They felt soothing to her feverish hands. She was going to die today, she was certain of it. So far, her daughter had shown no signs of radiation sickness at all. She prayed she had judged correctly, assuming the nuns would show her daughter kindness and take her into their monastery until it was her turn to die.

* * *

Very few people were watching TV when the special report came on. The elderly Lee's were in their graying first-floor apartment. Mrs. Lee was wiping down the small wall shelf that served as their ancestral worship shrine. Mr. Lee was pouring tea from his ceramic teapot into his tea bowl, just as he had every morning for 40 years. The old man's studied sips of the hot, yellow liquid were interrupted by the sudden light and noise of the television coming back on. Mr. and Mrs. Lee stared at the image of the young reporter running into the newsroom, waving a small square of white paper. The reporter sat down at the desk and with a slight puff still in his voice read aloud. "Central Government would like to apologize for the inconvenience resulting from the false alarm that sounded at Kuo-Sheng Nuclear Plant, affectionately known as No. 2. This incident has been put down to human error."

Mr. Lee put the teapot down and reached for the remote control. Mrs. Lee abandoned her cleaning and sat on the worn leather sofa next to her husband.

"Inconvenience? What inconvenience?" Mrs. Lee asked. Her husband hushed her with a flick of his hand, as he pushed the "volume up" button on the remote control.

Unable to suppress the realization of his own

good luck showing on his lips, the young newsreader looked right into the camera and continued his update.

"It seems there has been an explosion in the Hsue-Shan tunnel. Built in 2006 and at that time the fifth-longest tunnel in the world, it had just completed its 20-year check. Preliminary investigations indicate that there was a tremor, causing groundwater to pour into the system. Both entrances were partially blocked by rockfall, and have now been sealed against further flooding for the protection of all citizens. It is believed the convoy of buses heading to Yilan after the incident at Kuo-Sheng plant are inside. At this stage, it is not known when or if the tunnel will be accessible to robotic equipment to search for survivors."

Mr. Lee stood up and hitched his thin cotton pajama pants up to his chest and tied the cotton string tight. Putting on his thick white-soled rubber slippers, he shuffled to the door, telling his wife, "I am not surprised. I need to tell Pei-Ling about the tunnel. Radiation sickness? Flooding? It's allergy to this damned government. That's what is going to kill us all."

* * *

In the tunnel, Mayor Chen was now standing in front of the mass of concrete that blocked the entrance. It was deathly quiet. There was no young woman's voice to tell him he would exit the tunnel in five minutes. There was no young boy's voice trying to convince him to show affection. There was no wife's voice to tell him to put on more clothes or drink more water. There was no president's voice to tell him he was making a fine sacrifice for the country. There was only the voice in his head, telling him he should have seen have the signs when the pills were handed out ten years ago.

Relying on the soft glow of reading lights that was still on inside the tomb-buses, Mayor Chen carefully made his way back to his bus and to his seat. With all the effort he could muster, he moved the comatose Hao-Ping to the aisle seat. After squeezing his middle-aged body between the two boys, he took his son's water bottle off his unmoving lap. He looked hard at his son. He was a good boy. He patted his head. His son would have liked that. Grunting a sigh, he put his thick fingers into his pocket and pulled out the little white box, now slightly soggy. He carefully took out the pill. It was still in tact, but tiny pieces of card from the box stuck to it where he had not dried it completely. The pill was now between his thumb and forefinger. Mayor Chen popped it onto his dry tongue. With shaking hands he opened the water bottle and drank a mouthful. The pill's smooth outer coating had dissolved the first time he placed it in his mouth, and now it stuck a little in his throat on the way down. Squeezing his eyes hard, the Mayor managed a forceful swallow.

Chen took one more gulp of water before

placing the bottle on the floor. Then, he reached back into his shirt pocket and pulled out his cellphone. Where was his wife? Perhaps she was still alive. The reception indicator was flashing between no bars and one. He would take a chance. With great effort, Chen found his wife's last text, reminding him to take care of himself. Fighting the darkness, Mayor Chen of Keelung pushed the "reply" key, and typed his final message to the world.

About the Author

Katrina A. Brown grew up on New Zealand's Wild West Coast and moved to Taiwan in 1995. Katrina's fiction and poetry explores people's relationships with the physical and social environments they find themselves in. Her work includes two children's books and many articles in Centered On Taipei, culture.tw and other on-line and print magazines. Visit her at kabrown.com or on twitter @kabrownauthor.

We'll See Each Other on Facebook

by
Edward Y. Cheung

The signs are written in Chinese, a language still alien to me, a white-bread boy from the South Bay suburbs. They pack the canyon-like streets tight as jellybeans in a jar, and like the four and five-story high buildings that line the Taipei streets, are streaked with the detritus of typhoon rains: mold and dirt deposited, it seems, decades ago. Though I cannot read their contents, I have an idea what they advertise, as the most prevalent things here on the street sides are: eating hovels, boba tea shops, 7-Elevens and Family Marts, cosmetology and barber shops, scooter repair garages and health clinics, all packed in tight and competitive, most mom and pop.

Signs, everywhere one goes. Everywhere swimming the humid air-sea, alien and indecipherable. Like the signs spread out across my soul that point I, Mikey Stevenson, in one particular direction: *home*. Back to my hometown of Campbell, California.

The packed in signs are symbolic of my biggest complaint with this city: the claustrophobic tightness of its streets. The people, the buildings, and the apartments all jam packed together. I prefer the airy, open neighborhoods of suburban California. Strip malls, open freeways, four bedroom houses, rolling golden hills, and mild summers. Here the weather's too close, the people rub too close, hell, even the crowds of scooters, taxis, and high rolling Taiwanese cats in Beamers and Audi's end up tailgating pedestrians because the city planners, geniuses all, forgot to add sidewalks.

I wasn't always this jaded. Or rather, I was, but in a different way: I was jaded by suburbia and I was jaded by my job. I first arrived here in June (six months back now), a refugee from the land of GodIHateMyJobVille. I was working as a business intelligence analyst (more of a data collector. A job that paid the bills, but which I now found staid and boring), and wanted to get away from all those boring jaggy line graphs, pie charts, numbers, and grids all laid out sterile on white screens. I wanted to get away from beige cubicle rattraps and bullpens under depressing, unnatural fluorescent lights. I wanted to escape the pressure cooker of rushing deadlines and especially that clawing, hollow feeling I got in the pit of my stomach the moment I parked my Toyota Camry in the exact same spot in the company parking garage, at more or less the exact same time to repeat the same routine I'd been following day in day out for the past two years. I wanted what most people in the world want at 26; excitement, adventure, the feeling of the exotic, of discovering something new. I wanted something out of left field. So I followed my Taiwanese buddy Peter Lin's suggestion, and decided to head off to Taipei (even though I'd never even been outside North America before). There I'd try to find a teaching job, and maybe take a couple of classes in Chinese.

That June, I stepped off that cold, vacuum-sealed 757 to be hit by a single whiff of packed in-humanity. And I felt what the great discoverers of the world must have felt perched at the edge of vast, undiscovered frontiers. That the world was ready to be mapped, explored, and perhaps conquered. And so I found myself out on the open road. Clear skies, and no traffic. A bank account full of cash, and a calendar free of responsibility. So I floored the accelerator. First week; in a hostel. I was alcohol-fueled, loosey-goosey-buzzed, and talking to everyone I could. I met expats from all over Europe, Asia, Australia, and North America. Some looking to settle in Taipei for a few months, and in between airplane and apartment, some only in town for a few days, and looking to stretch their travel budgets. With the Europeans it was a free flow of passable English – a discussion on governments, politics, and systems exotic to an American boy like me (how many parties fought for power in a European government? ...*crazy*. A universal free college education in most of these countries? ...*damn*). With the expats from the other Asian countries, it was stumbling, trippy, word-by-word sentences heavily accented. I also met with a Californian, and a New Yorker, and we became fast friends. But all of us, whatever country we were from, were free like leaves in the wind, and together we danced through the big town of Taipei.

With tall, lanky Julian, a nuclear engineering student from the University of Heidelberg. A cool cat -- simultaneously brilliant, worldly, and ready to party. Julian had a plethora of very 'cool' interests, from surfing to playing the electric guitar, to camping, to rave hopping, and so when we weren't out partying at the clubs and downing shots, we'd chat in the hostel common area, aside tables and sofas.

With a handful of college kids from other parts of the states, and one from Cali. With ABT's (American born Taiwanese), a lot of em' here for a few days and ready to party it up after a sweat-drenched day of sightseeing.

Under neon lights, we'd roll up to the high tech clubs (simple syllable places like: Myst, Luxy, Spark, etc.) in yellow Taipei taxis (fare on the cheap), along oil-slick streets, half-drunk with whiskey we'd imbibed on long comfy couches in the common area of the hostel. We'd get in line with those Taiwanese dudes in tight, dun black, grey, and red club shirts and jeans, their hair slicked and black. With women in miniskirts hitched up to the butt, stick thin legs protruding out, layers of SK2 whitening makeup to make their skin their porcelain whitest, accentuating mile-long fake lashes and meter high high-heels. Past the bouncers, and into *bump-bump-bump,* green laser light shooting everywhere, the close sweaty press of alcohol-fatigued, alcohol-fueled bodies, moving to the rhythm of the DJ shouting on the mike, as the bass sensations of house, rap, R&B, music, dance and hinting of sex pounded like primal war drums. The perversion of fluorescent into purple, green, hazed light sandwiched by the dark shadows of the club. Making out with anonymous pretty girls, rejected by anonymous pretty girls, trips back to the bar with throat-burning alcohol, beer, stumbling hot-drunk back to the peaceful, jet-black bunk of my hostel. And waking to daylight and trudging like hung-over zombies to find our companions lounging on the couch nursing similar hangovers, and how different we seemed then compared to our night selves during the day. The bite of bile in one's throat when we awoke. A laugh as we recounted how many times we overdrank and threw up, then lazy moments checking emails, Facebook to talk to friends old and newly made. The night's activities capped off with a quick, convenient trip to Seven or Family Mart, or the many, many eating hovels in the area.

During the remaining few hours of the day, Julian and other ad hoc groups of friends went out to other touristy sites around Taipei (recommended by hostel staff and the lovely Lonely Planet). These were the hours of our field education. We went to the National Palace Museum to look at ancient Chinese antiquities (bronze age war swords, porcelains from the Ming Dynasty), to get a primer on Chinese history and to let Mikey Stevenson know just how young his mother country really was. We went out to the Beitou hot springs to lounge in scalding water, steam puffing up into I and Julian's alcohol addled heads. Early evenings, we'd stroll around the night markets (Tonghua, Shida, Raohe); crowded thoroughfares lined by food stalls, restaurants and clothes boutiques. There, we passed iron grilles sizzling with meat-on-a-stick, oysters, shrimps, and mini-crabs. Noodles, soup, and stinky tofu boiling in vats of bubbling brown liquid. And all a third of the cost of the drive-ins and Chipotles back in the 'burbs'. The steam of cooked foods, and a hundred new experiences wafted into the air, over dirty tables, bowls, and chopsticks and stripped down to the basics of friends and food (no candlelit dinner and silverware here, no). All in a vacuum of time, for we lost track of what day it was and really didn't give a damn. But somewhere in the back of our minds, was the sense that these carefree days would end, and so we pushed harder, faster, fuller, drunk with life.

Sadly, those days came to an end with the beginning of the summer semester. Before I'd come to Taiwan, I'd decided to try my hand at Chinese. I'd need something to do during my foray into exotic lands, and at the time, I knew a grand total of one and an eighth (that eighth being my really spartan Spanish) languages. I wanted to throw myself into something far into the outfield. And Chinese was out into left field, past the bleachers, and several towns over. And wouldn't it be somethin', to see a white-bread kid from the suburbs chopping it up in Chinese, something to confuse the hell out of white and Asian folks alike. So when those rolling tonal syllables came fast and fluent out of my mouth, people would say...*woah*.

That was the idea at least, but sometimes things don't go the way you expect. Progress slower than planned. You might not get exactly what you imagined or wanted. Story of my life, actually.

May. The first day at Shida University, where'd I'd be taking classes. I walked past stone walkways L-ing past trees, neatly trimmed hedgerows, statues of university luminaries, and tall red-bricked buildings that held various University Departments. My target, however, was the Department of Chinese Language Studies. And I gladly stumbled out of the baking summer heat (30 Celsius, wet shower of humidity) and into the crowded university halls. I zigzagged through presses of international students from all over the world, from the Asian triumvirate of Japan, Korea, and Vietnam, to the United States, to Europe, to more exotic countries like Swaziland, Namibia, the Bahamas, and some I'm sure, from extra-solar Alpha Centauri. Past inter-country clusters laughing and mingling until the four times *dunn-dunn-dunn-dunnnn* of the school bell – very distinct in Japanese and Taiwanese countries.

Sometimes in hindsight, you wonder what could have been if the Fates had thrown something else your way.

This time, Fate threw me into a classroom composed entirely of Japanese and Koreans. As I stepped out of the gray Formica hallways, and the sounds of alien languages, I entered a dull, gray, windowless classroom, with its 80's desk benches, single-watt florescent track lights, and powdery, stained whiteboards. Our class would be led by Ms. Lin, a tall, gangly, bespectacled woman in her early 40's from the outskirts of Taipei, who was single, and firmly – by Chinese standards – in cat woman territory. My classmates included 2 Japanese girls from the provincial areas of Kyushu Island: tall, pale Yuki, with her with her bowl hair-cut, porcelain white skin, and fragile constitution, and her friend Madoka, short, and diminutive as a twig. Throughout the semester, bound by more traditional social mores, they would maintain a reticent silence, and when they did speak, haltingly, shy, and half-whispered, I'd have a feeling that each word uttered was triple cross-checked for appropriateness. Then there was Yen, a cool-chill slacker from Osaka who chain-smoked his way through the semester. He was the type of guy who'd sit on a bench, and stare off into space people-watching, observing the motor scooters zoom by for hours at a time. And finally, there were the two Lees; Won Lee and Yoon Lee; two huckster types who happened to have the same last names like brothers, acted like brothers (as they huggy-felt and slapped each other on the back and sat bromance close with arms around the shoulders), but who were actually not brothers.

With my classmates, the synergistic relationships happened in pairs. Impenetrable force fields bubbled around Yuki and Madoka, The Lee Bros, and to some extent, I and Yen. Yen spoke a little bit of English, which was enough for us to have simple conversations about things like food, movies, and homework assignments. Because of the language barrier, we were consigned to chilling out together, not thinking too much, watching the class around us, sharing a cigarette in front of the 7-Eleven convenience stores, watching the world go by. A far lighter friendship than the friendships I'd had back home.

Mornings were spent in class, afternoons and evenings in the apartment. Nights were spent with

Julian and Yen (I'd introduced the two) in the neighborhood parks or bars sharing pints of Taiwan Beer. We'd shoot the shit over cuss words in different languages, drinking games, and on occasion, politics – but only when we got really drunk. I did a few of the assignments, and skipped many more, and our clubbing days had dwindled down to non-existence owing to the fact that all our former clubbing compatriots were busy with homework assignments or teaching jobs, or were tourists that'd only been around for a few days. Lunches were the socialization hour. I'd head on over with Yen and ad hoc groups of students, to sample a smorgasbord of food options near the campus (what would it be today? Beef noodles? Pizza? Salad? Dumplings? Wontons? Pot-Stickers? Ramen? Rice? Korean? Hamburgers? Cheap Sushi?). This was our school life, in my mid-twenties.

Then one day, in mid-September, I threw down a red 100 Taiwan-dollar bill on the counter of a convenience store to discover the cash pouch of my wallet vacuumed out. And a quick trip to the ATM made my eyes bulge.

Friggin money. Friggin reality. I didn't have enough money to cover rent the next month.

A remembrance of my apartment. It was a third-story studio in the center of the bustling Shida Night Market. 12000 NTD a month, habitation beginning after the first week at the hostel. It was dim, with wood parquet floors, a stunning view to the back of another apartment complex, and boxes of air conditioners sticking out from grimy windows. A squeaky mattress, a tiny desk strewn with papers from my Chinese class, empty beer cans, and my laptop with Excel uninstalled (for it reminded me too much of my previous job, and every time I thought about my previous job, I'd have to drink a few cans of Taiwan Beer to kill the pain.) And no kitchen, as cooking was wholly unnecessary in Taipei with the glut of cheap food being sold from open-air markets and restaurants. Spartan as the apartment was, rent was eating into my savings, and damned if the money hadn't gone quick on nights out at the clubs and bars.

I was going to have to find a job, and for a guy with my dirty blonde hair, pale, white-bread face, and reasonable command of the English language, that meant teaching English. Since I wanted to avoid teaching/babysitting kindergarten kids like the plague, I ended up teaching a business English class tailored toward local professionals. Familiar with business terms and concepts from my time at UC Irvine, I'd spend 12 hours a week teaching, with about 4 hours left for prep work. The hardest part of the job was dealing with a precocious 19-year-old Taiwanese kid – Lai (*the Professor*) – who'd ask millions of questions about the business models for various countries back home (from Google, to Berkshire-Hathaway, to Wal-Mart, and Chevron), questions I'd have to answer with: *"ahem, not sure. I'll tell you some websites that might have that info"*.

Life became routine, and peaceful, with the seldom stress of class and work. Life became...all right, sedated. Three hours in the dungeon of class. Off to lunch, then afternoons moping around, watching TV, surfing Facebook, staring into school assignments, or in Yen's case, space. Evenings prepping for work, then work, then perhaps a beer in the park, or at home alone, then sleep. We were becoming settled in our ways. School-adults.

But peaceful as the days were, when I came back to the empty apartment after a lunch with the fellas, I'd feel something in the pit of my stomach; something in the still of the desk, the chair; a silent cry that registered over the *vrrrr-vrrr* of scooters cutting through the street below, through the bursts of mirthful Chinese from the university kids strolling about.

What I felt was loneliness, the need for deeper companionship. Love.

I'll be the first to admit it: Mikey is an average looking dude. 5'7. Brown hair, pale, freckled skin, olive green eyes. Think a shorter Seth Rogen without the curly hair and a bit of a paunch 'cause even though I'd go to the gym on the weekends, I'd had the metabolism of a bear in hibernation. I'd never been popular with women, and the last relationship I'd had ended amicably when my girlfriend decided she wanted a change (from the endless toil of spreadsheets, the nights throwing on Netflix), and decided to run off to UCONN to get her MBA. So I was single when I came to Taipei, and on those clubbing nights, all those nights buzzed and sloshy, all those days walking the corridors of Shida University, my eyes wandered over to the pretty girls. Skinny girls from Asia. Bigger boned but equally fit girls from the European Union. Wondering, *Was she single? Should I chat her up? Easy, right? Say 'hi', where are you from? My name's Michael.* Often, I'd take action, striking out more often than not. (And how did I know? For a while, the conversation with (insert Japanese, Korean, or Chinese here)-girl would seem to be a-flowin'. The girl would giggle, smile, pay me a compliment on how great my (insert Japanese, Korean, or Chinese here) was ('cause I'd uttered a single broken greeting in her language – 'annyanghaseyo', 'ohayo'), and banter with me in halting English. But when I asked her if she was free for a coffee or to hang out, or to have dinner, she'd answer 'Sorry' or 'Sorry, I have boyfriend,' and then retreat into her classroom, or gaggle of friends. And that would be that.

A semester and a half of rejections. Single, along with Julian and Yen. Crashing into language barriers and cultural differences. But those lonely days would end and eventually lead to my undoing in Taipei. All because of a local girl named Sakura.

Because no matter how many times a social guy like me swings and misses; if he comes up to bat enough times, he's gonna hit. And the plate in this case was the Revolver Bar, a divey expat hangout about a 15-minute walk from the

University. Brick walls, bench tables accessorized with ashtrays, cigarette butts, pints of draft Taiwan Beer and Asahi, a small bar area filled with low to middle tier alcohols (your supermarket variety gins, rums, vodkas, etc.). On the bar stools and chairs were parked the butts of European and American expats, and the locals who wanted to meet them. Free spirits, mingling and friendly, clinking pints and cocktails. And that's where, on a Saturday night out with Julian and Yen – just chillin' -- I met *her*.

She was sitting with her best girl friend next to the table where I, Julian, and Yen were yammering about the eccentricities of our native languages (Swiss-German, English, Japanese) over a plate of savagely decimated nacho bits all gooey with sour cream gore. Frothy pints of Asahi at our chests. There she was, 150 centimeters tall (that's 5'0"), stick skinny in her five-inch heels, half-inch lashes, and blue contacts. Tiny chest, bone-thin arms jutting out from the sleeves of her slinky black cocktail dress, and layers of makeup that probably weighed more than she did. What I remember of her was that she was bubblier than a bottle of shaken champagne. Curtain of black hair to the lower back, flat nose, moderately slitted eyes hidden by those mile-long-lashes, face a natural tan because that was what most Western expats preferred, and a Union Jack tattooed on her lower back.

So I had to talk to her. When there was an opening, I turned her way, looking casually past the lines of her lashes and said.

"Hi, I'm Michael. What's your name?"

"I'm Sakura." Cigarette butt between the lips, puffing curls of smoke into the air.

"Nice to meet you, Sakura."

"Where are you from?" Her English was decent. Slow, smooth, with a tinge of a British accent thrown in .

"America."

"Oh! From the East Coast?"

"From California."

"Oh! The West Coast. I have many friend there. What are you doing in Taiwan?"

"Ah, nuthin' much. Learning some Chinese, I guess. Trying to figure out what I want to do with my life."

"*Really?*" And at this her eyes widened, and for the first time in a very, very long time I felt like I had a captive audience. And then she broke out the Chinese. "*Ni. Ke. Yi. Shuo – zhong-wen-ma?* (Can you speak any Chinese?)"

"*Yi-dian-dian.*" A little. A handy word to memorize, especially when they asked you if you wanted any hot sauce on your food.

"Maybe I can teach you Chinese."

"That would be awesome," I said, and threw a smile full of Colgate-scrubbed pearls. "What do you do Sakura?"

"I am Japanese teacher."

"Really? So you studied Japanese?"

"Before, I study in University. And *go...* I mean *went* there many time."

"Wow...your English is so good! *Sugoi-ne!*"

A blush. *So she was bit shy. And*, I'd thought, studying the tiny line of her button nose, the deep black of her eyes, *very cute*.

"No, it's very bad," she said.

"It's good, trust me," I smiled again. "Wow. You know Japanese, and your English is so good. You must be very smart."

"No. I'm not. I just like to try different language. And travel. And shop. Like all girl." She laughed.

"Haha, yeah, it's universal, huh? Where do you like to travel?"

"Oh, everywhere. I have been to Europe, and New York, and Boston, and many times in Japan. And you?"

...And so it went. That evening, she had to take her friend Xiao-Bing (*'just call her Pepper'*) back home to her folks, so we exchanged Facebook contacts, Line Chat IDs, and cell phone numbers. Our first date was at a Starbucks close to the University, followed by many more Monday through Friday dates to night markets and mom and pop coffee shops. As the summer bled into Fall, and the weather cooled, we took more exotic trips out to the Maokong tea fields, bike rides near the Taipei Gongguan riverside, a day trip out to the hot springs of Wulai, and one particularly memorable trip to the beaches of Fulong where I got a sand castle's worth of grit in my ear. On those days, we played and soaked in the scenery, and swam, and ate, and biked, and hiked. I didn't care about a thing in the world then. The only thing was how much I loved being with this girl. I'd never met a girl just like her; so affectionate, so...*interested* in everything I had to say. I ended up seeing Julian and Yen less and less ('*sorry, spending time with the gal tonight*') and with my new companion I laughed, blabbed on and on 'bout many things; even told her a lot about mom, an English teacher, and dad – a hard driving tech executive. I talked about my native town of Campbell. Talked about strip malls, and open freeways, traffic jams, cineplexes, and hockey games, giant hamburgers, and the melting pot back home, with the Filipinos, Vietnamese, Cantonese, Taiwanese, White boys, and Black boys, and Mexicans. And she'd listened with rapt attention as we shot through those weekends.

Sakura was warm, affectionate, and a little bit crazy. A girl who could shop, and eat, and run around, then go clubbing late into the night. Who never, ever got tired. She still lived at home with her mom, but could come and go as she pleased. My formerly lonely apartment became enlivened with her presence, and on those nights when she wasn't around, I thought I could feel her Sakura-scent of lilac and orchids soaking into the floor, the walls, my desk, the sink of my bathroom, into Mikey Stevenson. Though we'd only known each other for a month and a half, I was ready for the long term, ready to stay with her many more months, to twine together tighter, deeper.

Then one night in late October, after we'd both come back from a night market dinner, watched some TV, showered, and had twenty minutes of quickie sex, I announced :

"Baby, tuition deadline's coming up. Gotta decide...gotta decide if I want to stay another semester."

In the grey semi-dark of the apartment (never pitch dark because of the buzzing market below), I could feel the rise and fall of her chest; see her eyes, so different than when she had on her makeup. I could feel her mind whirring.

"Or...?"

"I dunno. Go back I guess," and then I proceeded, hesitantly. "I was thinking...my lease is up next month. I was wondering...y'know, I'm having an awesome time with you. I just...love how I feel around you. You make me feel more...y'know, *alive,* than I've felt in a very long time. I'm thinking...I'm thinking...if it's ok with you, you can come to my place more often. Maybe move out of your parent's place and stay with me."

Silence. It was as if that proposal had sucked away all the frenetic energy of our screwing.

"Mm," she gave a quiet murmur, and said nothing more.

"What do you think?"

A long pause, and in the silence, I could hear my heart toppling.

"I think about it, ok?"

"Sure, baby," I said (even though what I wanted to do was heave a worried sigh). "Take your time."

I could sense that that night was the beginning of the end.

Up till then, I'd seen her once or twice on the weekends, and a couple of times during the week (she had a hectic schedule teaching Japanese students, and often met up with a bunch of her local and expat friends). The next week, when I met her for lunch at the local burger joint, she seemed distant, offering single word responses to everything I said (none of the usual excitable chatter, none of the rapt attention). And we sat and poked awkwardly at our strings of spaghetti, and picked at the bits of pepperoni and sausage on our pizzas, and I had no idea how to proceed. I knew something was up, but I didn't press her. Instead, I asked how her classes were going, how were her students, how were her friends, and hoped things would return to their theme park rhythms. I was convinced we could meet more often, and in that time I'd convince her to stay with me.

Little did I know quickly the end would come. That very same Friday, she swept the rug out from under my feet.

Me: So what are your plans this weekend, Sakura?

Me: Was thinking about seeing a movie
S: Mikey-baby...
S: I am Sorry. I have been thinking a long time...
S: And what I want to say is...
S: I like you but I think, we can be good friend.
Me: Good friends? What's that mean?
S: we can be good friend.
Me: you mean...JUST friends?
S: yes.
Me: I can't do that. I want to be more than that.
S: u mean more then friend?
Me: yeh
S: then I'm so sorry Mikey. we can't continue.
Me: but I wanna be with you Sakura. I've never met anyone like you. I wanna stay with you. I wanna be with you for a long time.
S: I'm sorry Mikey-Baby. But I am dating with another person.
Me: Now? You're dating other people NOW?
S: Yes. Michael. I'm so sorry.
Me: Have it your way.

...And so it went. I blocked her Line, de-friended her on Facebook, and took her mobile off my contacts list. That night was the last time I spoke with my boisterous Sakura. After that, I avoided most of the places we'd visited. I sat in bed for hours in the lonely silence, staring at the ceiling in the dark with a feeling of gnawing desolation in my stomach. I mourned. I missed her smell, her laugh, her voice. Feeling that she, along with the possibility of a future together, had been erased.

I somehow ended up reconnecting with Julian and Yen over brewskies at the Brass Monkey (not at Revolver; *nooo way*. I might see her there with god-knows-who-else-she-was-dating). I was a shell of a man with distant eyes, with my mind playing over and over again one particular image; of her at the tea restaurant overlooking the Maokong tea fields, those vast, verdant fields, green and full of life. A porcelain tea cup in one hand, as she brought it to her lips, and sipped languorously, and she laughed in delight as her tongue hit the Puerh tea, and the sunset hit her face at just the right angle, changing her liquid brown eyes to gold, then I thought: *I wanna be with this girl, I really do. I wanna know everything about her.* And no wonder the other girls at Shida, and on the streets had faded into the background, a white noise behind the Sakura who'd taken center stage in my world.

Images of her plagued me all the way until the end of November. It was the end of the semester; 00:00:00 for a lot of folks, including me. Julian's exchange program was coming to an end, and he'd be heading back to Switzerland in early December. Yen had run through his savings and was going back to Japan to seek gainful employment (probably as a waiter). So I had to ask, what was left for me here? Of the remainder of my Chinese class, only the Lee bros were continuing, and I was beginning to miss the comforts of home:

the In-N-Out burgers, the New York Steaks, the hearty American Portions, the fresh salads and sandwiches, the giant supermarkets and mega-stores and Wal-Mart's. My Xbox One in the roomy living room and my plush white couch and carpet. Sane weather. My buddies from work and school. The million varieties of beers to buy and shoot the shit with.

And most of all Sakura's rejection of me had somehow changed the city. The streets were corridors of melancholia, the sunsets stiff with mourning and loss. So I had to leave, I *had* to. I would not be continuing the semester. It would be *au revoir* to this little country in the Pacific -- perhaps forever.

And so, as the semester ended, we said our goodbyes in the way expats thrown together in one great melting hot pot did: over drinks at Izukayas (Japanese style bars) with draft Sapporo's and greasy meats on a sticks. Over hot pot dinners, with raw slices of meat, vegetables, and seafood dumped into boiling pots of broth. We talked about our plans (would we return? What kind of job would we be looking for back home?). Felt a sharp melancholy as we hugged and waved goodbye to our classmates.

Most of which we would never see again.

The signs.
The bus to the airport.

Today is my last day in Taipei, and they are the last things I see before leaving this world... this moment in time. I take one last look at a sign in English – red lettering on alabaster white. This one says in English: 'The People Make The Place' (an advertisement for an English-language school claiming to have the best teachers), before I turn to my slick black Samsonite suitcase, packed to the zippers with the clothes, souvenirs, kitchen utensils, textbooks, and other knickknacks I'd cleared out of my third-story studio over the night market. The one thing I didn't have were keepsakes of her. I had only her image, tucked away safely in my mind.

My Samsonite I toss into a compartment next to the bus wheel-wells, and it joins all the other suitcases arrayed out in the steel metal luggage cage. Compatriot travelers, on their way to different worlds.

Breathe.

Climb up the grated steps of the bus, past the doors, into a vinyl bus seat, and away from the heavy smells of the foodstuffs everywhere; the hint of smog that has, whether I'm aware of it or not, soaked into the oxygen in my lungs, into my blood so that when I get home my bro would remark; *you smell like Asia, dude.* And that's not the only thing. Some sloughing of personality from Julian, Yen, and yes, of course, Sakura has latched onto my own, like three more rubber bands to the Mikey Stevenson rubber band ball.

I slip on a pair of headphones, to Green Day's 'American Idiot.'.

An hour bus ride. Out of the city, and onto freeways surrounded by lush tropical greens, the sky blue, yet somehow somber. I stop off at the Taoyuan International Airport to roll past sterile open-atriums with arched skeletal frames, check-in counters, boarding gates where most everyone is in movement. Harried and rolling their bodies to those gate portals to other worlds, other stages in their lives. And momentarily I join the mass, teleported courtesy of United in partnership with Eva airlines back to the burbs' and away from this place which was somehow, detached and yet, intimately mine. Taipei and the people I'd left behind in that slice of time.

Ah well, I think, as the 757 lifts from the runway and I find, despite my melancholia, my body and spirit soaring to the tune of home...Campbell:

We'll see each other on Facebook.

About the Author

Edward Y. Cheung hails from the sunny, rolling hills of the Bay Area. He has spent some years abroad in Hong Kong and Taiwan, and loves the energy of those cities. He enjoys reading and writing fiction of all genres, and playing and programming computer games. When he is not immersed in creative worlds, he can be found in a pair of shorts, running up and down the rolling trails in his hometown of Castro Valley.

Glossary

All terms are Mandarin unless otherwise stated.

Ah-gong/A-gong – Taiwanese term to address an elderly man, particularly a grandfather.

Ah-Jie – "Ah" is a Taiwanese term of affection, usually for people younger than the speaker. It is used with the second character in the first name, in this case, "Jie".

Ah-ma/A-ma – Taiwanese term to address an elderly woman, particularly a grandmother.

Ai-yo – Expression of pain or surprise.

Ba/Ba-Ba – Father.

Di-Zi-Gui – *Standards for being a Good Pupil and Child,* based on the teachings of Confucius. Historically taught in schools, it is a guide to being a good citizen and living in harmony with others.

Ge-Ge – Elder brother. Used in families instead of names, or by anyone to address any male who is older than the speaker.

Ma/Ma-Ma – Mother.

Mei-Mei – Younger sister. Used in families instead of names, or by anyone to address any female who is younger than the speaker.

Shida – National Taiwan Normal University.

Shi-Jang – Mayor.

Shui-jian-bao – Pan-fried buns usually stuffed with pork and cabbage, leek, or vegetable with vermicelli. It is a popular Taiwan breakfast.

Suao – Mid-sized seaside town in northeast Taiwan, famous for cold springs, seafood, and surfing.

Taida – National Taiwan University.

Wai-guo-ren – Foreigner.

Yi-dian-dian – A bit, a little.